BEWARE!!
DO NOT READ THIS
BOOK FROM
BEGINNING TO END!

Summer vacation on an island! You're psyched for bike rides, windsurfing, and hanging out on Cat Cay's beach. There's just one problem. You hate cats — and Cat Cay is overrun with them. And there's something very creepy about these cats. . . .

Then your brother Sam disappears in the middle of the night — when the cats rule. You've got to find him! Do you look in the old lighthouse, where the crazy light-keeper has set up deadly booby traps? Or do you search the rest of the island — and find out the horrifying truth about the cats of Cat Cay?

This scary adventure is about *you*. You decide what will happen — and how terrifying the scares will be!

Start on Page 1. Then follow the instructions at the bottom of each page. You make the choices. If you choose well, you'll live. You may even learn the secret of the cats. But if you make the wrong choice . . . BEWARE!

SO TAKE A DEEP BREATH. CROSS YOUR FINGERS. AND TURN TO PAGE 1 TO *GIVE YOURSELF GOOSEBUMPS!*

READER BEWARE —
YOU CHOOSE THE SCARE!

Look for more
GIVE YOURSELF GOOSEBUMPS adventures
from R.L. STINE:

R.L. STINE

GIVE YOURSELF

Goosebumps®

NIGHT OF A
THOUSAND CLAWS

AN
APPLE
PAPERBACK

SCHOLASTIC INC.
New York Toronto London Auckland
Sydney New Delhi Hong Kong

A PARACHUTE PRESS BOOK

ISBN-13: 978-0-590-40034-3

This edition is for sale in Indian subcontinent only.

First Scholastic printing, June 1998

Reprinted by Scholastic India Pvt. Ltd., January; March 2008, January; August 2010, November 2011; July ; August; December 2013; August; December 2014; August; November 2015

Printed at Shivam Offset Press, New Delhi

You step off the ferry and take a deep whiff of the salt air. All right! you say to yourself.

Your parents rented a cottage on Cat Cay for the summer. It's an island near Nantucket. You're sure this vacation is going to be cool!

You stroll down the dock to the line of waiting taxis. Your twin brothers, Donny and Sam, race ahead of you. "Watch the boys," your mother calls to you.

You roll your eyes. Or maybe the vacation won't be so great. How come I always get stuck with the brat twins? you wonder.

Your mom and dad help a cabdriver load your suitcases into the trunk. You all pile in and your mom gives directions.

The driver's eyes widen. "You're staying at the Madd house?" he asks.

"The what?" you gasp.

Why would he call your summer cottage a mad-house?

Turn to PAGE 2.

"Are we really staying at a madhouse?" Sam asks your mother.

She laughs. "Don't be silly. That's the owner's name. Katrina Madd. We rented her house."

As you settle into your seat you glimpse the cabdriver's face in the rearview mirror. He wears a very worried expression.

You peer through the cab windows. Cottages line the sand-swept streets. High sand dunes with tall grasses lie just beyond the buildings.

Perched along the top of the dunes sits a row of cats.

Dozens of them. Watching the cab drive by. Just staring.

You stare back and shudder. You've never liked cats. They're so unfriendly. And they always seem to be up to something. As if they have some kind of secret.

Like those cats there, you think. They all have their noses up in the air as if they're *so* special.

As the cab winds through the town, you notice something strange. Even though it isn't late, all the shops are already closed. You watch people hurry into houses and pull down the shades.

The last of the light disappears with the setting sun. And you realize — the streets are absolutely deserted.

Turn to PAGE 3.

"I guess not much happens here at night," you comment.

Your mom gives you a squeeze. "Don't worry! You'll have plenty to do."

The cabdriver catches your eye in the rearview mirror again. He shakes his head once. Slowly. Sadly.

What is with him? you wonder.

Now that you've left the town, there are almost no lights anywhere. Finally you arrive at your summerhouse. Your family unloads the car.

As you head inside, the cabdriver tugs at your sleeve.

"Let me give you a warning, kid," he whispers. "Watch out for Katrina Madd. And never go out after dark."

You feel a chill. "Hey —" you begin.

But he doesn't give you a chance to ask him to explain. He hops into the cab and zooms off into the night.

Turn to PAGE 4.

4

You shake your head. "Katrina Madd can't be any stranger than that guy," you mutter.

Something rustles in the bushes. A moment later a huge white cat leaps out. It arches its back and hisses at you.

You can't help shrinking back. Maybe that cab-driver was right. Even the *cats* don't want you out after dark.

"Okay," you tell the cat. "I'm going inside. Sheesh!"

You follow your family through the doorway. Almost immediately the screen door bangs open again behind you. You whirl around.

A tall woman wearing a long white dress stands in the doorway. Her white hair is piled on top of her head. Her glittering green eyes gaze at you.

"I am Katrina Madd," she declares. "What are you doing here?"

That's weird, you think. Wasn't she expecting us? And where did she come from? She appeared out of nowhere.

"My parents rented the house —" you begin.

Katrina cuts you off. "Of course. Now I remember." She gives you a long stare. "We'll be seeing each other again."

Then she leaves, melting into the darkness.

"Not if I can help it!" you mutter.

Turn to PAGE 5.

You head for the dining room. Your mother is setting out plates while your dad makes sandwiches. The twins pour sodas.

"I just met Katrina Madd," you announce. "Is she ever a weirdo!"

"That's not a very nice thing to say," your mother scolds. "But I *have* heard that she's kind of a recluse."

"So is her brother, Jacob," your father adds. "He lives in the lighthouse at the ocean's edge. Katrina lives in the caretaker's cottage down the beach."

"They sound scary," Sam complains.

"If you don't bother them, they won't bother you," your dad says.

"No problem," you declare. "I'm going to stay far away from both of them!"

After a quick dinner, you all settle into your rooms for the night. Your parents take the master bedroom on the first floor. You've chosen a room upstairs with a view of the lighthouse. The twins share the room across the hall.

You've just turned out your light when Donny bursts into your room.

"Sam disappeared!" he cries.

Turn to PAGE 6.

"Sam disappeared?" you repeat with a groan. "Mom and Dad will go ballistic!"

"Don't tell them!" Donny begs. "We'll get in trouble."

You glance out the window. You spot a small figure running toward the lighthouse. "I think I see him," you tell Donny.

"Let's go get him ourselves," Donny urges.

You sigh. "Okay. Let's go."

You grab a flashlight. Then you and Donny creep down the stairs and sneak out.

A sharp scream suddenly pierces the night. You and Donny freeze. The hairs on your arms prickle.

"Sam!" Donny gasps.

Was it Sam? Is he in trouble?

You remember the cabdriver's warning: Don't go out after dark.

Why not? you ask yourself. What is out here in the shadows?

You gaze around, trying to figure out where the scream came from. The wind and water make it hard. You point at Katrina's cottage far down the beach. "I think the scream came from there."

"No," Donny argues. "It came from the lighthouse!"

If you think the scream came from the lighthouse, turn to PAGE 41.

If you think it came from the cottage, turn to PAGE 48.

The three of you bike into town. As you pedal along the sandy road, you glimpse dark shapes creeping through the tall dune grasses.

Cats. Black cats.

Are they following you?

Don't be dumb, you scold yourself. Why would they do that?

You ride down the town's main street. You and the boys peer at the different stores.

"Let's go fishing!" Donny cries. He heads toward a store renting fishing gear.

"No!" Sam pedals to the other side of the street. "Jet skis! Oh, please, please, double please."

You sigh. Great. No matter which you choose, one of the twins is going to pout and whine.

SCREECH! SCRRREEECCCHHHH! Brakes squeal loudly behind you. You smell burning rubber as several cars skid.

You check to be sure Sam and Donny are okay. Good. They're standing beside their bikes on opposite sides of the main street.

The cars are stalled in the street at odd angles. You can't figure out what caused the near-accident.

Then you see two black cats strolling across the street.

Turn to PAGE 68.

At last you're seeing the terrifying creatures that have been tormenting you.

The cats pouring through the door are hideous mutants!

Hundreds of twisted, all-white, bulging-eyed creatures writhe in the sudden light. You stare in horror as the horrible beasts screech and howl.

"They're not ordinary cats at all!" Sam gasps.

"They're *monsters*!" Donny screams.

You can't believe your eyes. Extra eyes, extra legs, mouths where noses should be — these mutants are the most horrifying things you've ever seen!

Go to PAGE 45.

"Okay, Sam. We'll try jet skiing." You and the twins head over to the store to rent the jet skis.

On the way across the street, several black cats pass in front of you.

"Shoo!" You wave them out of your way.

"Meow," the largest one replies.

"Same to you," you snap. The cat's smug face annoys you.

You and the twins enter the store. The owner takes you out back and sets you up with jet skis and life jackets.

But no matter how many times you try, none of the jet skis will start. You all just keep falling into the water.

The owner scratches his head. "That's strange. They were all working this morning."

"We'll try a sailboat, then," you decide. "Maybe we'll have better luck with that."

Did you say *luck*?

Turn to PAGE 98.

10

"Number ten!" you shout gleefully. "I remember it was the tenth step that was circled. Step over it, guys," you order your brothers. "Who knows why Madd circled it — but I don't want to find out."

"Me either," Donny agrees.

The three of you carefully avoid stepping onto the tenth step. You continue up the spiral staircase.

When you climb up six more steps, you make a disturbing discovery.

See what it is on PAGE 36.

"Meowwww! Arrowl! YEOWWWWL!" You cover your ears to block out the deafening cries of the caged cats.

Scraggly paws reach out to you. You glance wildly around. Where can you run? Where can you hide?

But then you hesitate. The cats aren't baring their claws. They aren't hissing or flashing their fangs at you.

In fact, they don't seem evil at all. Just scared and hungry.

You venture closer to a wall of cages.

"Meow!" a gray cat cries. It almost seems to be trying to speak to you. "Meow!" it cries again.

You reach out cautiously and touch the gray cat.

It starts purring!

"They just want to be petted!" Donny exclaims. He touches the outstretched paws sticking through bars in the next cage. Sam does the same.

All of you hurry from cage to cage, petting the poor cats. Soon the yowling is replaced by the sounds of contented purring.

Except for the cat in the cage at the very end of the row. It isn't purring. It's whining — in a voice that sounds almost human!

"Me-out! Me-out! Me-out!" it cries.

Go to PAGE 59.

Your mom and dad step out of the elevator!

"Mom! Dad!" Sam and Donny shout together.

"What are you doing here?" you add.

"We could ask you the very same question," your mom answers. "You're up earlier than the birds!"

"We — uh — that is . . ." you stammer. You glance over at Jacob. How can you explain any of this?

"Oh, they've just been here helping me out around the lighthouse," Jacob Madd declares. "I'm Jacob Madd. Welcome!"

Your mom smiles at Mr. Madd. "As long as they don't bother you while you're working." She turns to you and your brothers. "Dad and I were looking for you kids. We have a little surprise for you."

"A surprise?" You grin. "What is it?"

"This!" Mom holds out her hands.

"Oh, no!" you, Donny, and Sam all exclaim together.

"Meow," says the little white kitten in your mother's hands.

THE END

Piercing howls come from the other side of the door. You watch in horror as the wood splinters. Dozens of claws poke through.

You start to panic. You've got to stop them! But how?

You glance around and spot a thick sheet of wood. "Help me move this in front of the door!" you order the twins. "This should keep them out!"

Together the three of you lift the heavy wood and lean it up against the splintering door. This gives you a chance to take a better look around.

You take a deep breath to try to calm down. Panic won't help, you remind yourself.

There's glass all the way around the circular room — except for the door. A small streak of moonlight shines through the glass like a laser beam. Your eyes follow the windows around the room. Then you see it.

"There it is!" you exclaim. "The light!"

Go to PAGE 111.

"Why would Mr. Madd want us dead?" Donny sputters.

"I don't think he does," you respond slowly. "He's not after *us*. Did you notice that all the traps hit about a foot off the floor? They're not aimed at people. They're aimed at cats."

"Yeah, well, they almost got people. Us!" Sam declares.

"I want to get out of here," Donny whimpers.

"In a minute." You peer around the room. "Maybe we can find something that will help us fight the cats."

Your light shines on Jacob Madd's desk. The surface is covered with papers. A middle drawer stands half open. Bingo!

You check for unexpected flying objects. The coast seems clear. So you cross to the desk. Right on top you discover an envelope. It's taped shut. Scrawled across the front is the message: OPEN IN CASE OF EMERGENCY ONLY.

You shift your weight onto your other foot. Immediately a spiked steel bowling ball rolls toward you. You jump out of the way and grab the envelope. "That was close!" you gasp.

"T-too close," Donny stammers. "Isn't this an emergency?"

If you open the envelope, go to PAGE 125.

If you keep searching Madd's desk, turn to PAGE 24.

You wrap your hands tightly around the rope. The eyes are advancing quickly up the stairs. You've got to escape!

"I've got the rope," you tell Sam and Donny. "Donny, you hold on to Sam. Sam, you hold on to me. On the count of three we're swinging over to that doorway."

The boys grab hold of each other and you. "Ready!" they say.

"One. Two. Threeeeeeeeeeee!" You jump off the step and swing. For a few seconds you're swinging through the air like Tarzan on his favorite vine.

The breeze blows by you. Your pulse races. You only hope you aimed right! If you didn't, you'll smash right into the wall!

Swing to PAGE 38.

16

"We should follow those paw prints," you declare. "They'll lead us right to Mom and Dad."

You and the twins hurry down the stairs. You peer out.

Good. No sign of the giant cat.

You dart along the trail of paw prints. "I think they lead right back to where we saw that army of cats," you whisper.

You're right. In a few moments you and the twins are back at the dune. "You guys stay here," you instruct them. "I'm going to try to see what's going on down there."

You scramble to the top of the dune. The torchlights burn brightly enough for you to see your parents lying on the sand. They're surrounded by dozens of cats.

A heavy weight suddenly topples you to the ground. You twist around, gasping — and see a whiskered white cat face. Two green eyes glare into yours.

It's Katrina!

Turn to PAGE 82.

Katrina the cat-woman smiles out at you from behind the wheel. "What's the matter? Fare too high?" she asks.

"How — but — you —" you sputter.

"I know you were expecting George. But it's a funny thing," Katrina purrs. "No one in this town will drive after dark."

She narrows her glittering green eyes at you. "Now get in!"

You're too terrified to run. Too terrified even to speak. Your legs shake as you climb into the backseat. The twins slide in after you.

Katrina speeds away down the dark road. You wonder where she's taking you. But you're afraid to ask.

Looks like the cat got your tongue!

THE END

18

Trapped in a pit with an angry panther seems like an emergency to you!

You tear open the "Emergency Only" envelope with shaking fingers. If only it helps!

Inside is a clump of smelly herbs. It looks like dried parsley or oregano from your mother's spice cabinet.

You sniff it. Hey, you recognize that smell. It's the stuff inside cat toys.

"Yes!" you exclaim. "Catnip!"

Go to PAGE 101.

The cats writhe on the ground. They shriek and scream.

Then they begin to shrivel up into dust!

You can't stand it. You squeeze your eyes shut.

When you open them again — the cats have vanished! All that's left are a few wisps of grayish smoke. They quickly blow away on the dawn breeze.

Your parents rush over to you. They help you out of the pit, then throw their arms around you. "You saved us!" Mom cries.

Sam and Donny run up. You're so happy you even hug them.

"Everything's okay now!" you declare. "It's all over!"

Katrina comes up. "Maybe yes, maybe no," she mutters.

You stare at her. She may be human again, but she's still weird.

You head back home. You're exhausted. And hungry! All that running around, all that terror — you've worked up an appetite.

Mmm. You'd love a great big steak. Or kibble. Just thinking about it makes your tail wag.

Tail?

Uh-oh . . .

THE END (?)

SKRITCH. SKRITCH. You whirl at the sound.

The cats outside are clawing at the door, trying to get in. Ugh! How creepy!

Your nose wrinkles as you check out the room. The whole place smells of dirty cat litter.

THWUMP. A fat Persian cat drops down from the windowsill. It sits at your feet and gazes up at you.

"Mrrow," an orange-and-black cat comments from the couch. A gray tabby strolls into the room. Gradually, more and more cats surround you. Staring. Waiting for you to do something.

But what?

Sweat trickles down your back. You don't like standing in the middle of a sea of cats. And you have a feeling they don't like you being here.

"More intruders!" Katrina Madd strides into the room. "We know how to deal with them, don't we, my darling kitties?"

"We're not intruders!" you declare. "We're trying to find our brother, Sam!"

"Did I *invite* you in?" Katrina demands.

You shake your head. "No. But —"

"I rest my case," Katrina announces, cutting you off. "You're guilty. Your punishment has already been decided."

Read all about it on PAGE 37.

"Get back in the dumbwaiter!" you shout at your brothers.

The platform is crawling with snarling, spitting, hissing creatures. Their eerie silhouettes glow a shadowy blue in the dim light above the door.

Sam and Donny turn and jump back to the safety of the dumbwaiter. You're right behind them.

There's just one problem.

The dumbwaiter is gone!

"Aaaahhhh

hhhhhhhhhhhhhhhh

hhhhhhhhhhhhhhhhhhh

hhhhhhhhhhhhhhh!"

Your screams echo through the shaft as you fall.

How far do you fall? It's impossible to tell, because your screams echo. And echo. And echo. Scream after scream.

Sorry, but this sounds like

THE END . . . THE END . . . THE END . . .

Donny and Sam help you drag the boat ashore. "Let's stay close to the water," you suggest. "That way if any more of those cats show up, we can dash into the ocean."

You and the twins trudge along the shore. High dunes prevent you from seeing inland.

How did the dunes get so high? you wonder.

You also wonder if you're heading the right way.

The wind howls. Sand swirls around you, stinging your face. You can barely see. "Sam? Donny? Are you still with me?" you call to the twins.

Sam grunts beside you. Then you hear Donny shout.

"Look!" he exclaims. "By the dunes! What is it?"

The sand blowing in your face makes it hard to see. You squint — and gasp.

The powerful wind is blowing the dunes away. And under the sandy mounds is a row of half-buried buildings.

Turn to PAGE 58.

That was a pretty *odd* thing to do. Maybe you shouldn't have opened Katrina Madd's cage.

"Me-out!" she wails again. She lashes out with a paw. Giant claws hook into your shirt.

"Ouch!" you cry as the claws dig through your shirt and into your skin. "Donny! Sam! Help me!"

The twins try to pull you back from Katrina's clutches. But she reaches out her other paw and snags the twins in one swipe!

Using her mutant strength, Katrina Madd pulls the three of you into her cage.

Then she leaps out, slams the door, and locks you in!

"Let us out!" you scream, rattling the bars desperately.

The cat-woman ignores you. You watch as she leaps from cage to cage, freeing the hundreds of caged cats. In a great furry mass, the cats stampede to escape this black pit of horror. Leaving you behind!

"Let us out!" you scream again. "Let us out!"

Katrina turns her almond-shaped green eyes to you. She almost looks as though she's laughing.

"Me-out!" she purrs. "You-in!"

THE END

You keep searching through Jacob Madd's desk. You might find some stuff you can use later.

You shove the envelope into your pocket. Then you grab a small screwdriver and put that into your pocket too.

You continue rummaging through the desk. Your eyes land on a newspaper clipping about Jacob and Katrina Madd.

"Hey, you guys! Look at this!"

The twins crowd around you. You read them the article, which describes the brother and sister winning a prize at the island's county fair for an automatic pet feeder. It seems Jacob is known for his fantastic experiments. People came from all around just to get a look at his latest inventions.

"Wait a minute," you mutter. You take another peek at the news photo of Jacob and Katrina.

Then you gasp. "That's not the Katrina Madd I met!"

Go to PAGE 119.

"A cemetery!" you gasp. There in front of you, half-buried in the sand, are dozens of old head-stones.

The three of you stare in shock.

"I don't like this place," Donny says shakily.

"What is a cemetery doing under the board-walk?" Sam wonders.

"The sand must have covered it over the years," you guess. "When the people in the town built the boardwalk, they probably didn't even re-alize the cemetery was here."

That explanation seems reasonable. At least it stops Sam and Donny from being too freaked out.

Now, if you could just stop *yourself* from pan-icking . . .

"What does RIP stand for?" Sam asks. "It's on all the tombstones."

"Rest In Peace," you tell him. You shiver. You don't want to stay here a minute longer. "Come on, let's keep going."

"But we'll have to crawl right through the cemetery," Donny complains.

"Tough luck. Move it."

The three of you start crawling again. But you've only covered a few inches when the ground falls out from under you!

Turn to PAGE 73.

You back slowly toward the garage, dragging the mouse on its string.

Katrina crawls on her belly, stalking it.

The plan is working!

You're inside the garage now. You give the rubber mouse a big tug. It scoots forward across the floor.

"Rrrrrow!" Yowling, Katrina bounds after it.

SLAM! The garage door slams shut. For once, the twins followed instructions.

Katrina's tail lashes. She pounces on the rubber mouse.

But she overshoots — and sails into the shelves full of cat food cans.

CRASH! The shelves topple over.

Blocking your way to the inside door!

You're trapped!

Turn to PAGE 87.

You duck down — just as a giant wrecking ball swings wildly across the room. It misses you by less than an inch.

"Whoa!" you cry. "What was that?" You turn to try to see where the ball came from. But there's no time.

"Look out!" Now it's Sam shouting a warning to Donny. Your eyes widen as a spinning saw blade flies through the air at knee level.

Donny jumps out of the way. "Hey!" he cries as a trip wire sends him sprawling. He lands on a conveyor belt, which starts up with a whir.

"No!" you gasp. Your heart pounds double-time. He's heading right under a guillotine blade! "Donny! Get up!"

But Donny lies frozen on the conveyor belt. His eyes stay fixed on the blade. He's too frightened to move!

You dash across the room. You reach for him just as he moves under the glistening blade. You grab his arms and yank him off the conveyor belt. The two of you tumble to the floor.

VVWHOOSH! The blade drops. Right where Donny's neck was only moments before.

"Jacob Madd is trying to kill us!" Sam wails.

Turn to PAGE 14.

You decide to stay in the lighthouse. Jacob Madd is one weird guy, but you would rather take your chances with him than go back outside.

Jacob hits a switch and the alarm cuts off.

"Whew!" Donny takes his hands off his ears. "That's better!"

"That alarm went off for a reason," Mr. Madd growls. "One of my booby traps must have worked."

"What do you mean, booby traps?" you ask.

"I —"

Suddenly the lights go out. You're plunged into total darkness.

At the window, you can hear the sound of claws ripping through the metal mesh screen.

You nervously peer into the dark. "What's that? And what happened to the lights?"

Jacob Madd gasps. "The cats are trying to get in!" he cries.

Go to PAGE 107.

The shining eyes of the cats advance quickly up the stairs.

The beam seems safer than the rope. "All together," you order. "We have to jump across."

You and the twins line up. On the count of three you all take a flying leap across to the beam.

Made it! You and the twins wobble a moment, but your landing is solid.

In fact, it's so solid that your weight makes the beam fold up like a Murphy bed! It fits snugly into a pocket in the wall. And it takes you and the twins along for the ride!

"Whoooooaaa!" you cry.

The beam snaps into place with a click. You and the twins tumble onto the floor of the lighthouse balcony. You feel around in the dark space.

WHAP! Your face hits a curtain. Cautiously, you pull the curtain aside and take a peek.

Into a room filled with cats!

Go to PAGE 105.

Katrina leaps for you. You twist and roll on the ground. "Missed me!" you shout.

You lunge for the hose. Donny and Sam race into the house.

You grab the nozzle. You aim it at Katrina. "Take that!" you cry, and squeeze the spray trigger.

Nothing happens.

Sweat beads on your forehead as you squeeze harder. Katrina crouches into a pounce position again.

You stare around frantically.

Then you discover what the problem is.

"Oh, no!" you moan. "The hose isn't hooked up!"

The hose isn't attached to the spigots on the side of the house. It is just lying in the grass.

It's useless!

As Katrina springs at you, you realize the true meaning of *cata*strophe!

THE END

"It's a ghost cat!" Sam cries.

Well, duhhh. You're in a ghost town — of course it's inhabited by ghost cats!

"Let's get out of here!" you shout. You and the twins dash down the main street.

And stop, terrified.

Hundreds of ghost cats fly through the air. They swoop toward you with their claws extended. Their howls and shrieks are deafening. Their eyes blaze with yellow fire.

Face it. On this island of evil cats, you never had a ghost of a chance.

THE END

You make a sharp turn. "Head for the board-walk!" you cry. The three of you dart across the sand. You scramble onto the weathered old boards.

"Aaaaaaggh!" The rotting wood crumbles un-der your weight.

You, Donny, and Sam tumble right through the floorboards. You land in a heap in the dirt under the boardwalk. Luckily, none of you is hurt.

Shrubs and bushes grow thickly on both sides of you. "How are we going to get out of here?" you mutter.

You glance up at the hole in the boards — and gasp.

Hundreds of eyes shine above you. Staring down.

"Cats!" Sam whimpers.

"Start crawling," you order. You hope the brush is so thick under the boardwalk that the cats won't sneak in.

You and the twins scurry along on your hands and knees. You can hear the sound of hundreds of little paws over your head.

After a while you notice the boardwalk is far-ther above you. You must be heading into lower ground. You don't care — as long as you keep a lot of distance between you and the cats.

Then you spot something ahead of you that sends chills up your spine.

Turn to PAGE 25.

"Look!" You point to the window. "The cats!"

"Help me stop them!" Madd drops the hose and throws his own body over the window to cover the opening.

But they squirm around, over, and under him. Cats and more cats pour into the lighthouse.

"Find the door!" you cry. But before you can grab the twins you hear a loud *THUD* and then a moan.

"It's Mr. Madd," Sam wails.

You grope through the darkness and find him lying on the floor. "My head," he whispers weakly. "I've hit my head."

Madd grasps your arm. He struggles to speak. "To . . . the light," he murmurs. "You must get . . . to the light."

Go to PAGE 55.

You grab the hammock from the twins. "Okay, we'll try to tangle her up in this."

The three of you dash up the stairs. You rush to your bedroom window.

Katrina paces in the yard below. "There she is," Sam whispers.

You hold the hammock out the window. "Just a few more feet this way . . ." you mutter.

The giant cat moves into the perfect position. "Now!" you cry.

And drop the hammock right on top of her.

"Mrrrooowww!" Katrina falls over with the weight of the heavy netting. She kicks and claws — but she only tangles herself up even more.

You and the twins race into the yard. You carefully avoid her sharp claws and teeth as you tie her paws together.

She's trapped!

Turn to PAGE 95.

"I agree with Donny," you decide. "Mr. Madd is hurt. It may be serious. We should go get Mom and Dad."

You remember that Jacob Madd locked the door. So you feel your way along the curved wall until you get to the window with the torn screen. Tufts of fur cling to the jagged edges of the mesh. You take a piece of the fluff and rub it between your thumb and fingers. It feels amazingly soft.

At least it will protect you from getting too scratched up by the torn screen, you figure.

You hoist yourself up and squeeze through. You turn back to help the twins.

Donny reaches up to the window screen. "It feels like powder puffs!" he exclaims, fingering a tuft of fur. He yanks it from the screen. He pretends to powder his face and neck with the tuft, then does the same to Sam.

Sam giggles and grabs some of the fur. He rubs it all over Donny, trying to tickle him.

"Quit it!" you snap. "This is no time to be fooling around."

As usual, they ignore you. Grumbling, you climb back in through the window. The tufts of fur tingle along your skin as you squeeze through the screen.

Turn to PAGE 117.

The spiral staircase stops in midair!

"Oh, no!" you cry. "This stairway goes nowhere!"

You shine the light around and discover a dark doorway in the lighthouse wall. It's strange, because there's no floor in front of the doorway. The stairway isn't even close to it.

A rope hangs down from above. But the end is so far up in the darkness, you can't see what it's attached to. Across from the door, a thick beam sticks out of the wall. Although it's within reach of the stairs, the beam doesn't seem to lead anywhere.

"I guess we should go back down," you tell Sam and Donny.

The twins are too scared to argue. They silently turn around and head back down the stairs.

Suddenly, Donny screams and turns abruptly. The flashlight falls out of your hand and lands with a *CRASH* below. The light goes out.

Go to PAGE 104.

"Wh-wh-what are you going to do with us?" Donny stammers. "And do you know where Sam is?"

She ignores his questions. "You know what to do, my pets," she instructs the cats.

Katrina Madd is really wacko, you decide. "Come on, Donny, let's get out of — whoa!" You stumble. Dozens of cats are nudging you and Donny down the stairs to the cellar!

"Sam!" you cry as you spot a small figure in the dimness.

Your little brother glances up from where he's unloading a case of cat food. Katrina must have captured him!

"Get to work!" Katrina orders. "There are a lot of chores when you have as many cats as I do."

"Chores?" you repeat. You gaze at Sam.

"That's the punishment," he explains. "She already called Mom and Dad. They were going to ground us for going out at night and sneaking into Katrina's house. But instead they all decided we have to do whatever Katrina says."

Now you know why Sam screamed. Do you have any idea how many litter pans you have to clean? Some vacation!

By the end of the summer, you're practically *catatonic!*

THE END

The wall looms closer and closer. The doorway appears right in front of you. You're going to make it!

Closer . . . closer . . . you're there!

You let go of the rope and —

"Aaaahhhh!" you scream as you rip through the black fabric stretched over the doorway. Your feet flail in the air. Your hands grasp at — nothing!

You didn't fly through a doorway to safety. It's a doorway leading straight outside. The walls of the lighthouse tower rush by you in a blur.

You, Donny, and Sam scream as you fall and fall and fall.

All the way down you know one thing:

You've reached the end of your rope!

THE END

You bang your flashlight on your palm. The light flicks back on. You peer at Jacob Madd. "He seems okay," you tell the twins. "Let's get to the light at the top of the lighthouse."

You hear more and more cats climbing in through the window. Why? you wonder fearfully. What do they want?

You flick the flashlight around the room, searching for the way upstairs. As the light plays across Mr. Madd, an old brass key pinned to his pocket catches your eye.

Sam leans in next to you. "Take the key!" he urges. "I saw him use it to open that door." Sam points to a door across from the spiral staircase. "Whatever is in that room is a big secret. He didn't want me to see what was inside."

"Maybe he keeps cat repellent in there!" Donny jokes nervously. "We could sure use some of that!"

Donny gives you an idea. "Maybe Madd keeps those booby traps he mentioned in there. Maybe we should check out that room."

Your dim flashlight beam picks up shadowy figures of cats slinking toward you. Whatever you do — do it fast!

If you take the key and explore the secret room, turn to PAGE 43.

If you climb the spiral staircase to get to the light, turn to PAGE 118.

"No!" Donny wails.

"Don't worry," you assure the twins. "We'll find them!"

"But why would the cats take them?" Sam asks.

You shudder. "I think it has something to do with what Katrina said about needing a new Keeper of the Cats."

You gaze out the window again. The paw prints seem to lead down the path toward the beach.

Then you spot the huge white cat darting around the corner of the house. Yikes! You slam the window shut and lock it.

Through the glass, you watch Katrina slink around the yard. She stops to bat at a flying insect. She behaves a lot like a regular cat — she's just much bigger.

"What should we do?" Donny whimpers.

You stare out the window. You could track the paw prints until you find where the army of cats took your parents.

But then what will you do?

Or . . . you could try to capture Katrina somehow. Then maybe you could trade her for your parents.

But how can you trap a giant cat?

Neither plan is great. But you've got to make up your mind!

To follow the trail of paw prints, turn to PAGE 16.

To try to capture Katrina, turn to PAGE 132.

"Let's check out the lighthouse," you decide. "It's closer. If Sam isn't there, we'll leave right away."

You and Donny race toward the lighthouse. You try to ignore the rustling sounds all around you. But you can't help yourself. You scan the shrubs

You shiver. Are those *eyes* shining back at you?

No way! It's just your imagination, you tel yourself.

You and Donny are panting by the time you make it to the dark lighthouse tower. Your flashlight beam illuminates an open window. Donny pulls himself up and squeezes in.

I hope this isn't a big mistake, you think. Ther you clamber in after him. You land inside with a soft *THUD*.

BRRRRRUUUPPP!!! BRRRUPPP!! JOUWOP! JOUWOP!

"Donny!" You have to shout to be heard over the blaring sirens. "We must have set off the alarm system. Let's get out of here!" You scramble for the window.

It slams shut, nearly smashing your fingers. A set of iron bars clangs down across it.

"We're trapped!" you cry.

"L-l-look!" Donny points to the other side of the room.

A huge, distorted shadow appears on the wall. The hideous shadow-creature stretches out its arms. Reaching for you!

Turn to PAGE 127.

"The sprinkler system!" you order Sam. "Flip the switch!"

CRASH! The cats are in! The pale moonlight illuminates their shadowy shapes. They rush through the broken door like a tidal wave of furious fur.

"Nooooo!" you cry. You shrink back.

They're going to trample you!

Sam reaches up and flicks on the black switch. A whooshing of water rushes through pipes. You cover your ears to block out the deafening sounds all around you. Floods of rusty liquid gush out of corroded spigots in the ceiling and walls.

"Help!" the twins scream. Water spews into the room. Higher and higher.

The cats sputter and yowl, trying to keep their heads above water. But it's no use. They're drowning. You beat them!

Uh-oh.

We're trapped in here with them! you realize suddenly.

The same thing is going to happen to you, Donny, and Sam!

The water reaches your knees. Your chest.

It's up to your neck.

Too bad you never learned how to dog-paddle!

THE END

"Quick," you whisper. "Let's get into the secret room."

You shudder, knowing there are now dozens of cats slinking around in the shadows. Watching you.

You try not to let the twins see how much the creatures freak you out. Intelligent cats! You shiver.

You remove the brass key from Madd's pocket and hurry to the door. The key fits easily into the lock. You shove the twins into the room and slam the door shut hard behind you. You hope none of the cats sneaked in with you!

Almost immediately the cats start scratching at the door. You saw what they did to the screen. You hope the wooden door will do a better job of keeping them out!

"Hurry!" you urge. "We've got to find something that will help us. Those cats could get in any minute." You shine the flashlight around the room.

It's obvious this secret room is Madd's laboratory or workroom. Sounds of humming, clunking, and rumbling come from strange gadgets that fill the room.

"Duck!" Donny yells suddenly.

Go to PAGE 27.

44

You have to act fast — before the cats break through the door!

You decide to try kicking the light switch on. You quickly brush off the rust and grease. Then you kick it to loosen it.

But no light comes on. Instead, a small door in the base of the lamp slides open. Inside is a panel with ninety-nine numbered buttons on it.

You figure you're supposed to push some of these buttons. But which ones?

You really wish you had some help here.

Hey. Maybe you do!

If you have the cards from Jacob Madd's secret room, turn to PAGE 75.

If you don't have the cards, turn to PAGE 78.

The mutant cats shriek and howl. You watch in horror as they claw each other, trying desperately to escape the light's beam.

"They can't take the light!" you cry. "It hurts them!"

"Look out!" Donny screams.

"Stampede!" Sam shouts.

The twins leap out of the path of the crazed cats. Shuddering, you keep the giant lamp focused on the awful beasts.

One button rotates the light to the left. You press it with a shaking hand.

Masses of cats flee. They hurl themselves through the glass windows and onto the balcony of the lighthouse.

You press another button and the lamp rotates to the right. In seconds all the windows are broken. Hundreds — no, thousands! — of mutant cats leap over the balcony. They hit the ground and race for the sea.

The shrieks of the mutants echo all over the island as they flee the light.

Go to PAGE 50.

You have a feeling those note cards are important!

You grab the cards and dash out of the booby-trapped room. As soon as your flashlight beam hits the outer room, you hear animals scurrying away.

You still haven't actually *seen* the cats. They seem incredibly skittish about being caught in the light.

Hmmm, you think. I wonder if —

"Hey! Mr. Madd is gone!" Sam exclaims.

You sweep the room with your flashlight. "He probably woke up and got out of this place. We should do the same thing!"

"Forget it," Donny advises, trying the door handle. "We're locked in."

Sam screams and jumps up onto the first step of the spiral staircase. "Something touched my leg!"

"Come on," you urge, following Donny up the stairs. "Keep going. But remember the drawing. The word 'down' was written by the tenth step. Step over it just in case that means something."

Sam and Donny do as you say. The three of you carefully step over the "down" step.

But when you get to step number sixteen you make an amazing discovery.

Turn to PAGE 36.

You don't get the chance to do anything.

Two giant cats bound into the yard.

"Help!" Donny and Sam scream.

Your heart pounds as you wait for the cats to attack.

But instead they rub up against you, Sam, and Donny, purring like crazy. The noise is as loud as a race car engine.

Gradually the terrible truth sinks in.

"Mom?" you whisper, horrified. "Dad?"

"Told you so," Katrina comments from her net. "Would you please let me out of here? I'm just a regular person again, now that your parents are the new Keepers of the Cats."

You're pretty upset at first. But it turns out that having parents who spend a lot of time as giant cats isn't too bad. They let you stay up as late as you want, since cats are nocturnal. And they're really into between-meal snacks.

Okay, so it's a little embarrassing when they transform into cats right in the middle of your school play.

But hey — nobody's *purr*fect!

THE END

"That scream came from the direction of the caretaker's cottage," you insist.

You and Donny hurry along the beach. The wind whistles through your hair. You shiver and pull up the collar of your jacket.

You glance at the water lapping up onto the beach. You gaze at the moon reflected in the waves.

And freeze.

The moon isn't all that's reflected in the glassy waves. Behind you is a long row of cats.

Another scream shatters the still night.

This time you recognize the voice.

That's Sam for sure!

Turn to PAGE 53.

You pull out the paper with the nine numbers on it. As soon as you see it you know what to do.

On the panel of numbers from 0 to 99, you press only the buttons that have the numeral 9 on them:

9, 19, 29, 39, 49, 59, 69, 79, 89, 99

As you press each button, it lights up.

Your finger is coming down on 99 when —

CRACK! The last layer of rotting wood splinters. Cats stream through the gap, hissing and howling.

"The cats are in!" Sam shouts. "Turn on the light!"

You press down on button 99.

The old lighthouse light flashes on — and you scream.

What are you screaming about? Find out on PAGE 8.

The room falls eerily silent now that it is empty of cats. Sam and Donny rush to the balcony.

"Come here!" Sam cries. "Look!"

You peer over the balcony and gasp. Thousands of white cat heads bob up and down in the water as the mutants frantically swim away from the island.

You squint as orange rays spill across the water. The sun is just starting to come up.

This horrifying adventure has lasted all night!

"You did it!" A voice behind you startles you. "You saved the island from the evil cats!"

Go to PAGE 71.

"I don't think we have a choice, guys," you tell the twins. "We have to trust her."

You untie Katrina's feet. "Don't make me regret this," you warn her.

"Don't worry," she assures you. "I'll be as sweet as a kitten."

"That makes me feel so much better," you mutter. "Now, how do we save our parents?"

Katrina stands and stretches. "The best thing to do is delay the ceremony. If it isn't completed before sunrise, it can't be done at all."

"But how can we stop them?" you demand. "They already have their victims."

"I'll bring you to the ceremony," Katrina says. "You offer to be Keeper instead of your parents. But I'll give you something that will prevent the transformation from taking place. By the time the cats realize they've been tricked, it will be too late."

You don't like it. But it's the only plan you have.

You take a deep breath. "Sounds good. Let's go!"

Turn to PAGE 112.

This guy hates cats worse than I do! you think.

Sure, cats aren't the greatest, but you wouldn't exactly call them *evil*.

"You'll have to stay here tonight," Jacob Madd declares. "You can't go out there after dark. Not with those cats around."

No way are you staying with this nut! You scan the room for a quick way out. Then your eyes widen in shock.

Cats stare in from every window!

Maybe Jacob Madd isn't so crazy after all.

You remember the cabdriver's warning. And all those shining eyes in the dark.

This is ridiculous, you scold yourself. They're just *cats*!

You jump when the alarm system goes off again.

"Oh, no," Madd gasps. "A cat must have gotten in somehow." He glances at the windows. "And they're gathering outside!"

Now you don't know what to do.

Would it really be safer to be inside with Madd?

Or should you make a break for it and run home?

If you grab the twins and leave, turn to PAGE 89.
If you stay in the lighthouse, turn to PAGE 28.

"Hurry!" you urge Donny. You pick up speed. So do the cats following you.

The cottage isn't much farther. You notice lights have come on in the little house.

By the time you reach the cottage, you and Donny are out of breath from running. You dash into the yard. The cats scamper beside you.

You knock on the door, panting hard. The cats swarm around you, flicking their tails. Growling.

"That's it! I'm not waiting." You push open the door and drag Donny inside with you. The door bangs shut.

"Wow," you murmur as you gaze around.

The whole house is decorated with pictures of cats! Cat curtains hang from the window. Cat magnets cling to the fridge. Pillows with cats rest on chairs. Little paw prints are stenciled across the ceiling.

"Katrina Madd *is* mad — mad about cats!" you declare.

Turn to PAGE 20.

The twins scramble into the tiny space. You realize you've stumbled into a dumbwaiter — a tiny elevator. You figure it's used to bring meals to the panther. Maybe you can hide in here long enough to figure out what to do next.

But before you have a chance to decide anything, the dumbwaiter starts rising! Up, up, up into the dark and narrow shaft you came down.

You feel around in the dimness. There are no controls.

You're helpless.

"Where is it taking us?" Donny asks.

Before you can reply, a screeching yowl fills the shaft.

"What was that?" Sam whispers fearfully.

"It's not the panther," you whisper back. "It came from above us. It sounded like cats. Hundreds of them!"

Go to PAGE 114.

"Get to the light? What light?" you demand. "What do you mean?"

Madd doesn't reply. The hit on the head knocked him out cold.

"Wha-what are we going to do now?" Donny stammers.

"He wants us to turn on the lighthouse light," Sam declares.

"Or maybe he meant that's the safest place to hide," Donny argues. "What if he doesn't want us even to touch the light?"

"I don't know what he means," you confess. "All I know is this place is crawling with cats. And they're definitely evil. We have to do something!"

"Let's go get Mom and Dad," Donny whimpers.

"We can't just leave Mr. Madd here with those cats," Sam protests. "We have to do what he said and go to the light."

The twins turn terrified eyes to you.

"Well?" Donny demands. "You're the oldest. *You* decide!"

If you think you should go get your mom and dad, turn to PAGE 35.

If you think you should climb to the light at the top of the lighthouse, go to PAGE 39.

"Hey!" you cry. You whirl around.

And come face-to-face with the cabdriver from last night.

"What are you doing?" he demands.

"What are *you* doing?" you retort. "Why did you grab me?"

"Don't you see that cat?" He points to a large black cat that's walking down the street. "He was about to cross your path. Quick! Go to the other side of the street."

You stare at the driver. Is he a total loon?

"Why should I be afraid to walk by a cat?" you ask.

He shakes his head. "It's not just any cat. It's a *black* cat. Black cats are evil. They bring bad luck." He gazes at the cat and shudders. "Never let one cross your path."

He hurries away. You stare after him.

Then you glance at the cat.

He's sitting right in front of the ice cream parlor.

"This is ridiculous," you mutter. "Come on."

Sam and Donny follow you into the store. You buy three cones. When you come out, you see the cat has vanished.

It's silly — but you actually feel relieved.

Now all you have to do is pick an activity!

To rent fishing equipment, turn to PAGE 120.
To try jet skis, turn to PAGE 9.

"Mom! Dad!" You burst into your parents' bedroom on the ground floor. You flick on the light.

And gasp.

"They're gone!" Sam wails.

Your eyes dart around the room. The place is a mess! The furniture is overturned and the blankets are shredded.

You notice the torn curtains fluttering in the strong wind. "The window is open!" you exclaim. You dash over and peer out.

Paw prints. Hundreds of paw prints in the dirt beneath the window.

Oh, no.

"The cats took them," you moan.

Turn to PAGE 40.

You stare at the weathered cottages poking out of the sand. You wonder how long the buildings were buried. And where did everybody go?

The wind dies down as suddenly as it picked up. The silence is eerie after the howling sandstorm.

You gaze at the moonlit town. It's like something you would see in the movies. But out here, on this strange island in the middle of the night, it's all too real.

Sam grabs your hand. "Let's go look!" he urges.

Donny grabs your other hand. "Come on. This is so cool!"

You aren't so sure. The ghostly town gives you the creeps.

But do you want your little brothers to think you're a wimp?

Donny and Sam drag you a few steps forward.

Are you going to explore the buried town? Or are you going to try to get home?

To continue on your way home, head over to PAGE 136.

To check out the town, turn to PAGE 67.

You rush to the large cage at the end of the row and shine your light on it. You catch your breath.

A strange creature gazes back at you. It has the body of a very large cat. The almond-shaped green eyes are cat's eyes.

But the rest of the face is definitely human.

And it seems very familiar.

"I can't believe it!" you whisper. "I think it's Katrina Madd!"

Donny and Sam hurry to your side. They lean in to get a closer look at the strange creature.

She reaches out a paw. "Me-out!" she cries. "Me-out!"

"She wants us to let her out!" Donny says.

"What should we do?" Sam asks you.

You think for a second. If this is Katrina Madd, then how did she get down here so fast? And how come she looked normal when you met her earlier tonight? Did Jacob Madd work some crazy experiment on her?

Or is this a trick the evil cats are playing on you?

The real question is, should you open this cage and let her out or not? There is only one intelligent way to decide: Think of a number between one and ten. Fast!

If you chose an odd number (1, 3, 5, 7, 9), open Katrina Madd's cage and turn to PAGE 23.

If you chose an even number (2, 4, 6, 8, 10), gather your thoughts and turn to PAGE 69.

"No way am I letting you out of that net!" you tell Katrina.

"Ever!" Sam adds.

"You'll regret that decision," Katrina snarls.

"So now what do we do?" Donny asks.

"We stick to the plan," you declare. "We let the cats know we have her."

"How are you going to do that?" Katrina demands. "They'll attack you as soon as they see you. You'll never get your message to them."

You never thought of that.

"You kids are really dumb," Katrina sneers.

"Hey," you snap. "Can you turn back into a cat? I liked you better that way."

"Hmmph." Katrina rolls over in the net hammock.

"She's right!" Sam wails. "How are we going to use her as ransom if we can't tell the cats we have her?"

"I'm thinking. I'm thinking." You pace around the room.

What are you going to do?

Turn to PAGE 47.

"Forget the screwdriver," you mutter. You've never been any good with tools.

The life preserver is your only weapon — and it's not much. You pull it off the wall and fling it at the mechanical saber-toothed tiger. Maybe it will slow him down for a moment.

His foot-long fangs sink into the Styrofoam ring.

And stick in it! Amazing!

"Yes!" you cheer. "Yes! I rule!"

As the beast tosses his angry head, trying to shake his fangs free of the ring, you search for your escape.

"Up there!" Sam shouts, pointing to a corner of the ceiling.

Donny is there in an instant. He pulls on a long string hanging down from a trapdoor. But a trapdoor doesn't drop down. Instead, a panel in the wall opens!

The three of you slip inside the wall. The panel slides shut just as the tiger gets to it.

BAM! You hear the beast slam full force into the panel.

"We did it!" Sam exclaims.

"We sure di — ahhhhhhhhh!" You take a step back — and start to fall.

Go to PAGE 83.

The dog biscuit crunches so loudly you're surprised the cats don't hear you.

"Ready?" Katrina asks you.

You nod. "You stay here," you order the twins.

For once they don't argue. They must be really scared.

You follow Katrina down the side of the dune. Hundreds of cats gaze up at you. But they don't attack. You guess that's because you're with Katrina.

You scan the beach. There they are — your mom and dad!

They're trapped in two small pits. Only their heads show aboveground. Cats pace back and forth in front of them.

"You're lucky," Katrina whispers. "They're about to start. Go for it."

You clear your throat. "I volunteer to be Keeper of the Cats instead of those two." You point at your parents.

A growl ripples through the army of cats. But then a large white cat nods. Dozens of cats nudge you forward. They shove you into a hole in the ground. Only your head pokes out.

You feel faint with terror. The ceremony is about to begin.

And your life depends on a dog biscuit!

Turn to PAGE 93.

"Quick!" you cry. "Up the tree!"

Sam and Donny don't have to be told twice. They scurry into the branches. You follow them.

Katrina grips the trunk with her claws. She chases you up the tree, growling.

But she outweighs all of you. As she places a paw on a branch it gives a loud *CRACK*!

Then the branch snaps off and falls to the ground, taking Katrina with it.

"Yes!" you cheer.

Katrina lets out a howl of frustration. You scramble through the window and slam it shut.

You're safe!

For now . . .

Turn to PAGE 57.

You take a seat by the throttle. Your heart starts beating at a normal pace again.

"That was so weird," Donny comments.

"No kidding," Sam agrees.

"Let's wait out here for a while," you suggest. "I don't feel like going back there too soon."

You cruise around the bay. But soon Donny and Sam begin to grow restless. It *is* kind of boring, just going around and around in the water.

But the cats still watch you from the dock.

"Why don't we check out that island?" you offer, pointing at a rocky mound in the bay. "It might be cool to explore."

You bring the boat around and head toward the neighboring island. You run the boat up onto the beach and scramble out.

You stroll down the beach with the twins. Sam suddenly gasps and tugs at your sleeve. Donny stands frozen, openmouthed.

"What?" you ask. You gaze in the direction Sam is pointing.

Your eyes widen.

Sitting high up in the dunes, watching you silently, is a row of . . . dogs!

THE END

None of the cats blinks. Or moves. They don't even seem to be breathing.

Weird!

You force down your terror. Time to take a closer look.

Cautiously, never taking your eyes off the closest creature, you creep out of your hiding place. You approach a large lion.

You burst out laughing as you realize the truth.

"They're stuffed!" you exclaim. You dash from one to another. "All of them are just stuffed cats!"

"Cool!" Sam exclaims. He and Donny dart out from behind the curtain. They start exploring the room, patting the stuffed creatures, and fooling around. Sam presses a button on the wall.

"Be careful!" you start to warn the twins — when you hear a horrible snarl behind you.

You spin around. And gulp.

You're face-to-face with a stuffed saber-toothed tiger.

Only now it's alive!

Go to PAGE 85.

"Mr. Madd?" you shout. "Mr. Madd? Where are you?"

No answer. Only a steady growling from the invisible cats. You feel their presence, even though you can't see them.

"The cats got him!" Sam cries. "We shouldn't have left him!"

Sweat breaks out on your forehead. These cats must be really dangerous!

What will they do to *us*? you wonder. Panic washes over you.

"Hurry!" you urge. "We're going up to the light. That's our only hope now."

You climb the first two steps of the spiral staircase. Then you stop. You're trying to remember the drawing on the note card. One of the stairs was circled and the word DOWN was written next to it. But which step was it?

You could kick yourself for deciding not to take the cards.

Think! you order yourself.

If you remember which step number was circled, step over to the page with the same number.

If you can't remember the number of the step that was circled, go to PAGE 135.

You can't resist. You have to check out the buried town!

"Okay," you tell the twins. "But stick together."

You and the twins scramble over what is left of the dunes. You hurry into what seems to be the center of the town. You gaze at the weathered old buildings.

"Awesome!" you exclaim. Moonlight dances across broken windows and half-open shutters. Many of the houses have old-fashioned porches. One has a large swing hanging from carved eaves.

"I wonder what happened here," Sam whispers.

A gust of wind blows a yellowed and torn newspaper down the street. You pick it up.

Your eyes widen as you read the front page. "This is from over a hundred years ago!" you exclaim.

You scan the headlines.

And feel a chill of horror.

Turn to PAGE 86.

The cats saunter to the curb. When they reach it, they sit down and begin to wash themselves lazily.

The drivers in the cars all stare tensely at them.

Did those cats somehow cause that accident? you wonder.

You shake your head. That's crazy. The drivers must simply have been trying to avoid hitting them.

The cars start up again. But you notice they peel off in new directions. Not one of them continues the way it was going.

Not one of them passes the cats on the corner.

You bike over to Donny, in front of the fishing shop. Sam reluctantly joins you.

"This means we're going fishing, doesn't it?" he demands. "I want to jet ski. Or go sailing."

"Well, I want to get some ice cream," you tell him. "Then we'll figure out what to do."

You chain the bikes to the low rail in front of the fishing store. You stroll along the street. You thought you noticed an ice cream parlor a few blocks back.

A hand suddenly yanks the back of your collar. Hard!

Turn to PAGE 56.

You chose an even number. You need another minute to think about this.

While you're thinking, you're startled by a voice from behind you. "I see you've found my sister!"

You whirl around. Jacob Madd is standing by the spiral stairs.

"Mr. Madd!" you sputter. "What are you doing here? I thought you were —"

"What you think and what is real are two very different things," Madd sneers. "You thought you were trying to get away from the evil cats. But really you should have been trying to get away from me! You see, I need you to finish my experiment."

"E-e-experiment!" you stammer. "What experiment?"

"Human-to-animal transformation," Madd replies. "Katrina is the closest I've come to success. Now I'll have three more chances to get it right. Are you ready for the change?"

Go to PAGE 131.

"Forget it!" you snap. "I've had enough cats for one night."

"You're no fun," Sam complains.

"Shut up — or I'll tell Mom and Dad you sneaked out," you retort.

You and the twins hurry home. You creep back into the house. Luckily, your parents slept through the whole thing.

"I just hope I don't dream about cats," you mutter as you climb back into bed.

The next morning is overcast and cloudy. Not a great day for the beach. "I'm going to ride my bike into town," you announce.

"Fine," your mom says. "Donny and Sam will enjoy that."

You groan. "Do I have to take them?"

"Yes, you have to," your mom replies calmly.

You sigh. Somehow, you knew how that conversation was going to end.

"Okay," you tell your mom. "But don't blame me if they get into trouble."

Your mom ruffles your hair. "Don't be silly. What kind of trouble could two little boys get into?"

You roll your eyes. Oh, please . . .

Turn to PAGE 7.

You spin around to see who is speaking. The light blinds you at first. But when you duck below the beam you discover Jacob Madd.

"Mr. Madd!" you exclaim. "How did you get up here?"

. "I took the elevator, of course!" He seems surprised by your question. He points to the elevator door behind him. "How did *you* get up here?"

You sputter in disbelief. You start to explain all about spiral staircases, secret rooms, and booby traps.

Madd interrupts you. "You took the long way up. If it hadn't been for that bump on the head, I would have told you about the elevator. But never mind that now. It's not important.

"For five years I looked for ways to get rid of the mutant cats," he continues. "I only figured out the importance of the light when I saw the cats run from your flashlight. I couldn't have done it without you. I —"

He breaks off as the elevator whines into life behind you.

All four of you stare tensely at the elevator door. Who could be coming up now?

Then the door slides open.

See who's there on PAGE 12.

"Let's get out of here!" you tell the twins. You slide down the dune. Then you scramble to your feet.

But you freeze when you hear a loud wailing sound.

You glance back.

Oh, no! Hundreds of cats swarm up the dune.

"They're after us!" you cry.

You, Donny, and Sam run as fast as you can. But it's tough going. Your feet slip and slide in the sand. Donny and Sam struggle to keep up.

You spot a boardwalk at the foot of the dunes. It leads in the direction of your house. It should be easier to run on the boardwalk than on the shifting sand.

But it's awfully dark in the shadow of the dunes.

You glance toward the ocean. A rowboat is pulled up on the sand. Maybe you should get away on the water. But — navigating a rowboat in the dark? You're not so sure.

But you *are* sure the cats are gaining on you. Do something!

If you head for the rowboat, turn to PAGE 109.
To run to the boardwalk, turn to PAGE 32.

"Aagh!" you scream. You're falling!

THUD! The three of you land in a deep, dark pit. You jump to your feet and throw yourself at the sides. But they're smooth, hard-packed dirt.

There's no way out!

You gaze up. Once again you find yourself staring into hundred of glowing eyes. Rows of cats crouch along the rim of the pit, preparing to pounce.

That's right. Any second, they're going to leap down into the pit. All is going according to their plan.

You should have taken a closer look at those headstones. Because at *this* cemetery, RIP stands for Ripped Into Pieces.

THE END

"Hurry! Let's climb out of this pit!" you whisper to Sam and Donny.

The three of you dig your fingers into the dirt wall and try to pull yourselves up.

"It's too slippery!" Donny cries. "I can't hold on."

He's right. You all slide back down the wall.

You jump up again. This time you dig your toes in too.

"Yaaahhh!" You're yanked off the wall by a sharp tug at the waistband of your shorts. The huge panther clutches your shorts in its teeth. It drags you down and releases you.

Donny and Sam huddle behind you. But you don't think you can protect them. Your legs tremble as you stare at the big black cat. It reaches out and bats at you with its paw, knocking you over backwards.

"Aaahh!" you scream. You fall into Donny. Donny falls into Sam. You topple over like a row of dominoes.

The black panther pounces and holds all three of you down. There's no getting up those walls now.

In fact, there's no getting up ever again.

For you, this black cat is just plain bad luck.

And for the cat, you're just plain good cat food!

THE END

Aha! You remember the note cards from Madd's secret room. You fumble around in your pocket and feel two cards.

You don't have time to make a mistake now. You've got to pull out the right card the first time. You reach in and . . .

Take two slips of paper. On one slip, write the words SPIRAL STAIRCASE. *On the other piece, write the words* NINE NUMBERS.

Put the two slips of paper in your pocket. Mix them around.

Now reach in and pull one out.

If you pull out SPIRAL STAIRCASE, *turn to PAGE 124.*

If you pull out NINE NUMBERS, *turn to PAGE 49.*

So it *was* Sam who screamed! He must have tripped the same alarms and gotten caught by this wild guy too.

"You mean there are two of you?" the bearded man sputters. He claps a hand to his forehead. "First those dag-blasted cats. Now the island is swarming with clones!"

You stare at the old man. Clones? He must be joking.

"We're not clones!" Sam exclaims. He starts laughing. "That's a good one."

"We're twins," Donny explains. "We're staying in the house down the beach."

The man lets the hose drop to the floor. He straightens up and adjusts his glasses. He pulls at his beard.

"The house?" he repeats. "That's my house. I'm Jacob Madd. Do you know why I don't live there anymore?" He glares at you, as if he's daring you to answer.

"Uh, no," you mumble. You wish he'd move back a bit.

Madd's eyes widen fearfully behind his glasses. "Because this lighthouse is the only place safe from those evil cats!"

Turn to PAGE 52.

You reach for the camera. But Donny clings to it. He shakes his head vigorously.

"It's my camera," he whispers. "I'll take the picture!"

You glare at him. But you can't argue. The cats might hear you! You have no choice but to give in.

Donny aims the camera.

CLICK! Flash! CLICK! Flash!

The flash! Oh, no! You forgot all about it.

If the cats didn't notice the clicking sound, they definitely caught those bursts of white light.

"Let's get out of here. Now!" you shout. You drag Donny and Sam down the dune.

Hundreds of furious cats chase after you. But you had a head start. Maybe, just maybe, you can outrun them!

Then Donny stumbles. He drops the camera. It pops open, ruining the roll of film.

"Noooo!" you wail. But you don't have time to yell at Donny for being so clumsy. Not with a hundred cats leaping at you.

Oh, well. They say a picture is worth a thousand words. But was it really worth your life?

THE END

Too bad. You don't have those cards.

You could kick yourself for not going back and getting them. But it's too late now. You'll just have to figure out for yourself which button to push.

Oh, no! The cats are almost in. You have to do *something*! Frantically, you push button number 1.

The glass walls whoosh open. Yikes! Cats pour in from the balcony.

"That was the wrong button!" Donny yells.

"No kidding!" you shout back. You jab button number 2.

This time, the ceiling opens up. "Aaaahhh!" You scream and cover your head as cats drop down from above.

"They're everywhere," you gasp.

Your hands shake as you reach for button number 3.

But it's too late. They pounce.

The cats have got you covered.

In fact, they've got you buried!

THE END

"Okay," you tell Donny. "Go get the camera. That way we'll have real evidence."

Donny rushes into the house. After a few minutes, he darts back out, waving his camera. "Let's go!"

"Be very careful," you instruct the twins.

You retrace your steps. It's easy to do, since you left a trail of footprints in the sand.

When you reach the dune, you take a deep breath. Your heart is hammering.

You nod at the twins. They nod back. You can't hear anything, but that doesn't mean the cats aren't down there. Waiting to pounce.

You and the twins creep silently up the side of the dune. You still can't believe what you see in the flickering torchlight. All those hundreds of cats. And there in the center — the giant white cat you know is Katrina.

You don't even want to *think* about what they might do if they discover you taking pictures.

Don't make a sound! Turn to PAGE 77.

You and the twins dash away from the dune. Away from the terrifying sight. And away from the unbelievable fact that you've rented a summer house from a cat-woman!

You might all be in danger. What did Katrina say to the cats? That it was time to find a new Keeper?

What if they decide your mom or dad would be perfect for the job?

You have to warn them!

"We have to tell Mom and Dad," you say to the twins.

"They'll never believe us," Sam argues.

"And we'll get grounded for going out at night," Donny adds.

Hmmm. The twins have a point. *You* wouldn't believe you if you announced you saw a woman turn into a cat.

At least — not without proof.

Is there a way you could prove what you saw? You're almost at the house. What will you do?

To tell your parents, turn to PAGE 126.
To find a way to get proof, turn to PAGE 88.

ART, CAPE, CAP, CAR, CARE, CART, CASE, CAST, CRATE . . .

You did it! You found at least nine other words hidden within SPIRAL STAIRCASE.

But there are so many more words to be found. You don't want to stop now. In fact, you get so into it that you forget all about the cats, the light, and the danger.

All you care about is this SPIRAL STAIR-CASE word search!

"Stop it!" Donny begs.

"We've got to turn on the light!" Sam adds.

But you can't stop listing word after word after word.

"Air, Ape, Are, Ace, Ate," you rattle off. "Eat, Ear, East, It, Is, Sir, Price."

"No! Stop!" Donny cries.

"Pace, Pest, Lap." Your list keeps growing.

"The cats are in!" Sam shouts. "They're ready to pounce!"

"Rice, Race, Rail, Real, Rat, Star, Sat."

You're still finding words. You can't stop yourself!

The room fills with angry cats. They tackle you and smother you in fur. But as your final breath leaves your body, you shout out one more SPI-RAL STAIRCASE word:

"LAST!"

And that's exactly what it is — your last word.

THE END

The big cat clutches you in her paws. You cling to her fur, trying to avoid her deadly claws. "Help!" you pant.

Together you roll down the sandy dune. You bang into a torch. It falls to the ground.

Cats scatter, howling. You and Katrina roll over the sandy ground, locked in your struggle. The screaming cats race about.

And then — you're falling! You tumble into a hole in the ground, taking Katrina with you.

The din suddenly stops. An eerie silence falls over the cats. They all seem to be waiting for something.

Red light touches the walls of your hole. The sun is rising, you realize.

A moment later Katrina transforms back into a human!

"You saved me! I don't know how — but you saved me!" she cries. She leaps out of the hole. "The cats did this to me!"

She jumps up and down joyfully. "The reign of the cats is over now. They can't stand the sunrise!"

You stare out of your hole. Is she crazy? Or is it true — the terror is really over?

Your eyes widen as you see what's happening around you.

Turn to PAGE 19.

"Aahh!" you shriek, falling down, down, down.

"Oh, noooooooooooo!" Donny and Sam cry together.

There's a musty smell in the air. Like the smell of a basement that hasn't been aired out in a long time. The further down you fall, the warmer it gets.

After what seems like forever, you land with a quiet *THUD.*

The three of you lie flat on your backs in stunned silence.

Then a terrifying sound makes your body tremble in fear. A steady growl begins very close to your ear.

You quickly roll away from the sound. You glance back.

And stare into glittering cat eyes.

Just enough light leaks down from above to show you a gigantic panther. A *real* one!

Donny opens his mouth to scream. Sam slaps one hand over Donny's mouth and one hand over his own.

The beast gazes at you. It licks its lips.

You struggle to think clearly. You remember the "Open in Case of Emergency Only" envelope.

Should you open it and hope whatever is in it saves you?

Or should you try to climb out of this pit?

If you try to climb out of the pit, go to PAGE 74.

If you open the Emergency Only envelope, turn to PAGE 18.

"Jacob Madd said we have to get to the light," you remind Sam and Donny, "and that's what we're going to do!"

You reach into your pocket and pull out the screwdriver. As hard as you can, you hurl the tool at the crowd of creatures guarding the door. "Take that!" you shout.

They scatter!

"It worked!" you cry. You feel a rush of triumph. "Run to the door!"

Sam gets there first. He pushes the door open just far enough so he can squeeze through without letting the cats in. You crowd in behind him and pull Donny in with you.

"Wait!" Donny cries when he's halfway in. "My sock! Their claws are stuck in my sock!"

The claws are pulling Donny out the door and you're pulling him in. His sock is stretched to the limit.

You're not going to let these cats stop you now! Not when you're so close to escape!

You give the cat's paw a hard smack to make it release Donny's sock. "YEOWWWWL!" the cat screams.

That smack was a big mistake.

Now the cats are mad!

Turn to PAGE 13.

"Look what you did!" Donny accuses his twin.

"I didn't mean to," Sam sputters, his eyes wide.

In front of you, the tiger flashes gleaming fangs at you. It slowly moves toward you, opening and closing its mouth.

Hey! Is that metal inside there?

Phew! This saber-toothed tiger is mechanical!

"It's not alive!" you declare. "It's a machine. It must be another one of Madd's inventions!"

"Machine or no machine," Sam cries, "it's coming after you!"

He's right! The mechanical menace stalks toward you. It seems programmed to kill! Sweat breaks out across your forehead as you stare at the big cat's foot-long fangs.

In one second, you think, we could all be shish kebab!

You glance around for some kind of weapon. You spot a Styrofoam life preserver hanging on the wall.

Could you use that somehow?

Or what about the screwdriver you took from Madd's office? It just might save you. After all, the tiger is a machine.

"Hurry!" Donny pleads. "Do something!"

If you pull the life preserver off the wall, go to PAGE 61.

If you'd rather use the screwdriver, turn to PAGE 90.

"Wild Cats Invade Wilson Cay," you read aloud. "Townspeople Flee."

So the cats drove the people out!

"This island used to be called Wilson Cay?" Donny asks.

"It looks that way," you reply. "Until the cats got here."

The twins stare at the newspaper in your hands.

"I'm scared," Sam says in a small voice.

"There's nothing to be scared of," you assure him. "There's no one here."

Or is there? You jump when you hear the porch swing squeak. It moves back and forth, back and forth. . . .

"Who's there?" you call. You try to sound brave.

Your heart thuds hard when you hear the answer:

"Meow!"

"Oh, no!" you groan.

A large gray cat leaps off the porch swing. Where did it come from? You could swear it wasn't there a moment ago.

It dashes past you.

And walks right through a wall!

Turn to PAGE 31.

"Donny! Sam!" you scream. "Open the garage door!"

They can't hear you. They're doing exactly what you told them to do — they're staying outside, out of the way.

But Katrina can hear you all right. Her ears prick up at the sound of your voice. She bounds over to you and swats you. Hard.

"Owww!" You sprawl onto the floor. She leaps on top of you.

"Get off of me!" you grunt. You manage to push her off.

Before you can scramble to your feet, she brings a huge paw down on top of you. She pins you to the floor.

She's *playing*!

This cat-and-mouse routine is a cat's favorite game.

Unfortunately, *you're* the mouse.

And this is

THE END!

You arrive back at the house. "You two are probably right," you decide. You stare up at the dark windows. "Mom and Dad will never believe us."

"I have a camera. We can take pictures!" Donny suggests. "Then we'll have proof."

It's a good idea. But you're not sure you want to risk going back to that army of cats. Isn't there some other way to get proof that Katrina Madd is a cat-woman?

You suddenly remember the cabdriver's warning.

Hey! Maybe he knows something. Maybe he would believe you.

Maybe he can help you.

That's a lot of *maybe*'s, you think. It might be better to go with Donny's plan.

To try to get proof by taking pictures, turn to PAGE 79.

To try to find the cabdriver, turn to PAGE 92.

"This guy is wacko," you whisper to the twins. "Let's go home."

You shove the twins in front of you and dart across the room. You fling open the door.

"No!" Jacob screams. "Shut the door! The cats! The cats!"

You and the twins dash outside. The moment the three of you are through the doorway, the door slams shut behind you.

Donny lets out a big sigh. "That sure was weird."

You don't answer. You're too busy glancing around, searching for signs of cats. What if Jacob Madd is right about them?

You're embarrassed to feel your heart pounding so hard. It's ridiculous to be so nervous about a bunch of cats!

"Look." Sam points toward the dunes. "It's a cat parade!"

Sam's right. A procession of cats makes its way over the dunes. The moon outlines their silhouettes.

"Let's find out where they're going!" Donny exclaims. He and Sam tug at your arms.

You can't help but be curious too. Freaked out — but curious.

To investigate what the cats are up to, turn to PAGE 116.

To keep heading straight home, turn to PAGE 70.

"Got it!" you exclaim, fishing the screwdriver out of your pocket.

The tiger's jaws open wide, ready to chomp down on you. Sam and Donny cheer from the sidelines as you dive through the tiger's legs. You slide under him.

Now you're behind him. You discover that bolts at the joints hold the beast's legs together. There's your plan!

The screwdriver fits perfectly. You cling to the tiger's legs as you work quickly to unscrew the bolts.

Done! You scurry out from under the mechanical beast as his hind legs collapse.

In a rage, he turns his huge head toward you. You sprint across the room.

But your moment of triumph quickly fades.

You can't believe it! The saber-toothed tiger still won't give up. Even dragging his useless hind legs behind him, he reaches you easily.

You're cornered!

Turn to PAGE 134.

Your heart pounds hard as you continue to stare at Katrina.

I can't be seeing what I think I'm seeing, you think. Katrina seems to be — shimmering!

She lets out a tortured wail. "Aaaaaaiiiii-ieeeee!"

Sam clutches your arm. Donny shoves his fist into his mouth to keep from screaming.

Your eyes widen in disbelief as you watch Katrina kneel on her hands and knees. She arches her back. She shrieks in agony.

And slowly begins a terrifying transformation!

Check out the results on PAGE 128.

"I know someone who will believe us," you announce. "That cabdriver. The one who drove us to the house."

"Great idea," Sam says. "But how are we going to find him?"

You rack your brain, trying to come up with an idea. You don't know the guy's name. You don't know where he lives. And it's the middle of the night. Hmmm.

Then you snap your fingers. "I know! We'll call for a cab! And we'll request someone who looks like him."

Earlier, you noticed a pay phone at the side of the road. You run to it and look up the taxi company in the phone book. Luckily, the island is so small there's only one.

You tell the dispatcher where you are. You describe the driver as best you can. She seems to know whom you're talking about. "He'll be there in ten minutes," she assures you.

You hang up. "I'm sure he'll help us!" you tell the twins.

You sit by the side of the road and wait. You keep your eyes peeled for any signs of cats.

Soon a car approaches. A taxi! You jump up and wave it down. As it stops, you, Sam, and Donny dash over.

You peer into the driver's window. And scream in terror.

Turn to PAGE 17.

One by one, cats creep up to you and breathe in your face. This must be the ceremony, you realize.

Your nose wrinkles. Ecchh! Cat breath.

Finally, the last cat breathes on you. The feline army forms a large circle around your hole. Watching. Waiting.

You wait too. Sweat beads on your forehead.

Did the dog biscuit work? Will it stop the transformation?

Will the sun come up in time?

Your head whips up to check the sky. Come on, sun, you urge silently.

There it is! Sunrise.

I don't feel any different, you think. You glance down at yourself. I don't look any different, either.

Yes! Katrina must have been telling the truth!

The cats let out a deafening wail. Agonized. The sound is horrible.

But the sight in front of you is even more terrifying.

See it on PAGE 19.

"All right." Your mom sighs, shaking her head. "But I can't believe they would just disappear like that without letting us know where they were going."

"You know how children can be," Katrina Madd murmurs. "Dashing here and there. Sometimes they just seem to vanish."

Yes. They do. Especially on an island filled with evil cats. With very special fur.

Oh, did someone *fur*get to warn you never to pet strange cats? And no cats are stranger than the ones on this island.

You aren't the first kids to pull a disappearing act — with the help of some feline friends. Er, foes.

Well, there's your future. Only you can't see yourself in it because — thanks to those cats — you're invisible.

THE END

You watch in amazed horror as Katrina the cat transforms back into a woman. She glares through the netting at you.

"Why did the cats take my parents?" you demand.

"The cats need a Keeper — a human they give the ability to transform into a cat," Katrina explains. "This Keeper feeds them, takes care of them, does anything they need. I was Keeper for nine years — but my time is up. So the cats took your parents to be the new Keepers. They decided they might as well take both."

"That's horrible!" you yell. "We have to stop them!"

Katrina's eyes glitter. "I'll help you if you let me out of this net," she promises. "I was made a Keeper against my will. I don't want that to happen to anyone else."

You laugh. Why should you trust her? "No, thanks. We already have a plan," you tell her.

"But are you sure it will work?" Katrina shoots back. "You don't have time for mistakes. Your parents may be transformed any minute. I'm the only one who knows how to stop it. Let me out!"

Could she be telling the truth? You glance nervously at Donny and Sam. They stare back at you.

Time is running out. Choose!

If you keep Katrina in the net, turn to PAGE 60.
If you let her out, turn to PAGE 51.

"Don't be dumb," you scold Donny. "Black cats can't give you bad luck. That's just an old superstition."

"Black cats?" The store owner turns pale.

Oh, no. Now *he's* going to get all weird on you!

"We'll take a motorboat," you say quickly. You turn to the twins. "That will be fun, won't it?"

Sam shrugs. "If we find one that works."

You follow the owner to a motorboat. "Get in," you order the twins. You really hope this time something will go right.

The motor starts up right away. That's a good sign, you think. The owner looks relieved. The twins cheer as you head out of the harbor.

"See? What did I tell you?" you cry. "Those stupid black cats can't —"

You never finish your sentence. Water suddenly begins to shoot up from a hole in the bottom of the boat. It gushes in so quickly you don't have time to call for help.

Before you know it, you're sinking!

Oh, well. Your luck just ran out. Glub, glub, glub!

THE END

The spiral staircase is about to take you completely underground. "Jump!" you shout.

Holding hands, all three of you leap off the tenth step. You land safely.

Much to your surprise, Jacob Madd stands a few feet from the staircase.

"Mr. Madd!" you exclaim. "What happened?"

Madd doesn't speak. You shine your flashlight at his face. You, Donny, and Sam gasp in horror.

Madd stands stiff and still as a zombie, staring straight ahead. His wide-open eyes are magnified by his thick glasses. His chest rises slowly as he takes long, deep, raspy breaths.

Long scratches trail down his cheeks. Shredded clothes hang from his stiffened body.

You gulp. What if whoever — whatever — did this to Mr. Madd is still here?

You have a bad feeling. A feeling that you know exactly who — what — attacked him . . .

A rustling sound behind you makes you jump.

Go to PAGE 110.

"You kids will have a lot of fun with this!" The owner instructs you on how to use the small sailboat. You and the twins clamber aboard.

Immediately the boat flips over. You flop into the water.

"That was fun!" Donny cheers. "Let's do it again."

"Let's not, okay?" you grumble.

You and the twins struggle to turn the boat upright. You scramble back on.

It flips over again. And again. And again.

"We're not having any luck with this," you tell the owner. "Maybe we should try something else."

"Let's scuba!" Sam cries.

The owner goes to find you the equipment. "Sorry. Out of luck," he informs you. "We don't have any gear in your sizes."

"Oh, man!" you grumble. "This just isn't our day!"

"It's the cats!" Donny declares. "Those black cats gave us bad luck."

Turn to PAGE 96.

"Run!" you cry. You grab each of the twins by the hand and drag them along the path. The house is just a few yards away.

Too late! A giant white cat leaps out of the bushes in front of you. Her ears flatten as she hisses at you.

"Katrina!" you scream. The twins duck behind you. You feel them trembling in terror as they clutch the back of your shirt.

The big white cat crouches down. Her eyes fix on you. You know she's preparing to pounce.

"Stay back," you tell her. As if she'll listen to you!

You stare at her huge green eyes, wondering what to do.

Then you spot a long hose lying in the grass.

Hey! Don't cats hate water? Maybe you can spray her long enough to get into the house.

There's also a large tree right beside you. Glancing up, you realize one of its branches brushes against your open window. Maybe you should climb to safety.

Hurry up and decide. That low rumbling sound isn't purring. It's an angry growl. Katrina is about to pounce!

To climb up the tree, turn to PAGE 63.
To go for the hose, turn to PAGE 30.

You didn't find nine words?

Maybe you just didn't try. If you didn't, then you certainly won't try to find the correct nine numbers to press on the panel!

Cats are lazy too. They love it when things come easily to them. And guess what just came easily to these evil cats?

YOU!

It's too late to change your mind now. Your own laziness has done you in.

The only words that might get you out of this now are these two:

THE END!

"How can catnip help?" Donny wails. He ducks to keep away from the panther's lashing claws.

"You'll see," you reply. You take a pinch of catnip and fling it at the panther's face.

The beast pauses, paw raised. You toss some more catnip at it.

Some of it lands right on the panther's nose. The big cat shakes its head, then sniffs the ground where more catnip has fallen. It glances up at you.

"Mrrrrow?" it says.

"See that?" you whisper to your brothers. "The catnip is making it happy!"

The big black cat flops down onto the ground and rolls around on its back. You toss a little more catnip over its face and the panther starts acting even sillier. Instead of coming after you and the twins, it swats at its own tail!

While the panther is playing, you slowly, quietly back away from it. Donny and Sam carefully step backwards too.

You back into something. A small closet in the wall.

"Quick!" you whisper to the twins. "Hide in here!"

Go to PAGE 54.

But Katrina Madd isn't dying.

She's transforming back into a human before your very eyes!

When the transformation is complete, she stands and faces you. There's nothing frightening about her now.

"Thank you!" Katrina cries. "You saved me — and all these poor animals!" She begins to release them from their cages.

"But what about Jacob Madd?" you ask.

Katrina points to the cage. Jacob Madd is gone. In his place, a white kitten meows gently.

"He knew this day was coming," Katrina explains. "One of his experiments backfired. He did something that was turning him into a cat. He tried everything to stop the transformation. He even experimented on me. I've been a prisoner here for three years!"

"Three years!" you gasp. "Then who's that woman in your house? The one who said she was Katrina Madd?"

"An imposter," Katrina says solemnly. "Jacob paid her to take my place. But now I'm back — and she'll have some explaining to do!"

Katrina leads you outside. You, Sam, and Donny start toward home. What a night! You're exhausted. In fact, you're ready for a little catnap!

THE END

"They're after us!" Donny screams.

"Scat! Shoo! Go away!" Sam shouts. As if that might do anything to scare these evil creatures!

Your heart races as you realize — the cats have completely destroyed the door. All that's keeping them out is one last layer of rotting wood on the plywood plank.

You've got to do something — or you're all finished!

Why did Jacob Madd tell you to get to the light? Was it because this is the safest room?

But if the cats can get in here, what's so safe about it? Your eyes search for a clue.

Did he mean the lighthouse light will save you? You could try turning it on — but will it work after all these years?

What did Jacob Madd want you to do here?

There's a switch marked SPRINKLER SYSTEM on the wall by Sam. Hey! Could the sprinkler system still work?

Maybe water will scare the cats away.

If you order Sam to flip on the sprinkler system switch, go to PAGE 42.

If you kick on the lighthouse lamp switch, turn to PAGE 44.

104

"Why did you scream?" you shout angrily at Donny. "You made me drop the flashlight!"

"I thought I saw one of those cats," Donny cries, trying to explain. "I mean, I saw a shadow. Honest!"

"It was probably your own shadow," you scold him. But when you glance past him you're not so sure. Are those two eyes shining in the dark? You squint, peering harder.

Uh-oh.

"The cats!" you yell. "They're coming up!"

"Where should we go?" Sam shrieks.

"What do we do?" Donny wails.

The only choices are to reach for the rope and try to swing over to the doorway in the wall — or jump for the old wooden beam sticking straight out of the wall.

This is no time to do eeny meeny miney moe. Just make your choice — fast!

If you jump for the beam, turn to PAGE 29.

If you think the rope looks more promising, go to PAGE 15.

"Oh, no!" Sam whispers. "The cats are here!"

The room is lit by candles in wall holders. The three of you survey it from your hiding place. Your stomach twists up with fear.

Hundreds of cats with bared claws and fangs stand ready to pounce and attack. The cats are all colors and sizes. There's even a saber-toothed tiger snarling in your direction.

They seem to be waiting for you to make a move.

Shaking, you stare at the horrifying creatures. And make a very strange discovery.

See what you discovered on PAGE 65.

106

You keep your eyes on the cat's tail. It's hard to tell exactly what it's doing in the dark.

"Oh, no," you murmur. You feel sick with shock and fear. Somehow, the cat has managed to open the window! Cats stream in.

You turn to warn the twins. You notice Donny has blown the largest bubble you have ever seen. It gives you an idea.

You grab the bubble from Donny's mouth. "Wha —?" he sputters.

You ignore him and hurl the bubble at the cats. It bursts on contact. Bits of sticky gum cling to the cats' fur. Angry hisses cut through the darkness. But the cats stop moving toward you.

"Blow bubbles!" you shout. "Throw them at the cats!"

Sam and Donny furiously blow bubbles. They fling them at the creeping creatures.

"It's working!" you cry. They may be evil, but just like ordinary cats they like to be clean. They're stopping to lick the gum out of their fur. This gives you time to gobble up some of the gum yourself. You chew, blow, and spit, chew, blow, and spit, trying to keep the cats stuck on licking themselves clean.

If you can just stall long enough, maybe you can escape!

Go to PAGE 108.

SKRITCH. SKRITCH. SKRITCH.

"We can't let them in!" Madd screams.

Your heart pounds faster. The clawing sound sets your teeth on edge. Especially since you can't see anything in the dark.

You flip on your flashlight. Madd aims the hose at the window. But no water comes out!

"Oh, no!" Mr. Madd cries. "The cats got to the water supply!"

What is this guy talking about? you wonder. Cats can't do something like that!

You run your flashlight beam along the faucet on the wall — and nearly drop the flashlight in shock.

"Paw prints!" you gasp. "They're all over the faucet!"

"The cats are intelligent," Madd whispers. "They've turned out the lights too!"

You flick your beam over to the light switch. More paw prints! Your mouth drops open in horror as the terrifying truth hits you.

These cats really *are* up to something!

Your light flickers and blinks out. "Stupid batteries!" you sputter, banging the flashlight on your palm.

But even without the light you can make out a creepy sight.

Cats are swarming through the hole in the screen.

Go to PAGE 33.

"Run for the door!" you order the twins.

But you don't get far.

The floor is covered with globs of gum. Your feet get stuck. Sam and Donny run right into you. The three of you tumble to the floor.

"Yecch!" you groan from the bottom of the pile. "I'm covered with gum!"

"So am I!" Donny cries.

"Me too!" Sam grunts with disgust.

No matter how hard you try to pull yourself up from the sticky floor, you can't move. You know very well what will happen next.

As soon as the cats lick themselves clean, they'll be coming to get you.

You'll keep trying to get away, of course, but one thing you're sure about now. Madd's Emergency Gum is the kind gum chewers stick with . . . forever.

THE END

"Quick! Get to the boat!" you cry. "Cats hate water."

You grab the twins and dash down to the rowboat. The cats race after you.

Panting, you shove the boat into the surf. Your jeans and sneakers get soaked. But you can't worry about that now.

The cats stop abruptly at the water's edge. They sit in a row — staring silently at you.

"So long!" you jeer. You're out of there!

"Where are we going?" Donny asks.

"To our house," you explain. "It's just down the beach."

You hope.

Soon you're sweating and panting. It's so hard to row in the gusting wind!

At last you spot a place to bring the boat into shore. You peer into the darkness, trying to see if there are any cats around. It's hard to tell — the tree branches quiver and shake in the wind, and the moon creates shifting shadows.

But you can't row anymore. You've got to risk it.

Turn to PAGE 22.

"We have to get out of here!" you shout. "The cats got Mr. Madd and we're next. Run for the door! Run!"

For once the twins obey you. They rush for the door.

ZZZZZZAP! A bolt of electrified blue light throws both boys backwards. Their hair stands straight up. Their arms and legs stiffen.

They must have stepped into some kind of force field!

You rush over. They fall against you. A shock of electricity surges through your body too.

You stand straight up, the twins leaning stiffly against you. Your eyes are wide open, just like Madd's. You can't speak or move — but you can still hear. You hear hissing and growling as shadowy cat shapes emerge from the darkness.

So the cats have won. They used one of Madd's own booby traps against you all.

As you stand there, shocked into stillness, you know one thing: You are definitely *claws*trophobic!

THE END

Donny and Sam rush to the enormous glass lamp stationed in the middle of the tower room. It's covered with a thick blanket of cobwebs. The bolts holding the light to the floor are rusted. The switches at the base are gunked up with grease and dirt. You can tell this lighthouse light hasn't been turned on in years.

You brush away the dirt from a switch. You're about to push the switch forward — when the sound of splintering wood stops you.

"Aaaahhhh!" Donny screams at the top of his lungs. You whirl around to stare at the door.

The cats have broken through the plywood! In seconds they'll be inside!

Go to PAGE 103.

112

Katrina leads you, Donny, and Sam over the dunes. The moon lights your path.

How soon is dawn? you wonder. Will we get there in time?

You gaze at Katrina. Is she telling the truth? Does she really have something that will prevent the transformation?

You shiver. All you can do is follow and hope.

And worry.

Katrina stops back at the dunes where you first saw her horrifying transformation. Your stomach flips over. Any minute your parents could be going through that same change.

Or *you* could!

Katrina hands you something. "Eat this," she instructs you. "It will prevent the transformation."

You glance at it. "A dog biscuit?" you sputter.

She frowns. "It's your only hope."

"Good luck," Sam tells you. Donny pats you on the back.

You swallow hard. Then you pop the biscuit into your mouth.

Hey! It's not bad!

Turn to PAGE 62.

"Hold on tight! We're going down!" you cry as the stairs spiral into the ground. They're carrying you into a pitch-black pit! From somewhere in the dark distance, the shrieks of animals reach your ears.

"What's that?" Donny demands, grabbing onto you.

You don't answer. You don't want to tell him — but you think it's the cats.

"We're slowing down!" Sam says.

"We're stopping!" Donny adds.

The cries and howls grow louder and clearer as your spinning stairs suddenly jerk to a stop. You, Donny, and Sam stumble onto a dirt floor.

Then, as fast as it carried you here, the staircase reverses direction. You're left in the darkness.

You flick your flashlight on and shine it at the wall.

Donny and Sam scream.

All around you the walls are lined with cages crammed full of hideous, twisted-looking mutant cats!

Go to PAGE 11.

114

Huddled together in the closet-sized elevator, you, Donny, and Sam can't do anything except wait to see what happens.

Seconds later, the dumbwaiter bumps to a stop, opening onto a small platform. The platform leads to a door. A small blue light over the door glows dimly. You can barely read the sign on the door: TO THE LIGHT.

"Hey!" you cry. "We're here! This is the top of the lighthouse!"

Donny and Sam leap out of the dumbwaiter and pull you onto the platform with them.

Then all three of you freeze. Your scalp prickles with fear.

Hundreds of pairs of cats' eyes glitter on the platform. Shadows hiss and creep closer to you.

The cats are blocking the door!

What are you going to do? You could try to get past them and to the light. Or is the dumbwaiter a better place to be now?

If you rush past the glowing eyes and open the door to the light, go to PAGE 84.

If you climb back into the dumbwaiter, go to PAGE 21.

Those cats are too creepy. You just want to get out fast! You decide to leave the cards where you found them.

You open the door and lead the way back out to where you left Jacob Madd. Hundreds of padded feet thump softly around you.

You aim the flashlight around the room, trying to see the cats. But it's no use. The shadowy shapes run from the light. They must only come out in the dark, you guess. You wish you could get a good look at them. It really freaks you out that you can't.

You cover the light with your hand. Then you quickly pull your hand away. Light washes over the room again.

But the cats aren't fooled by your light trick. They're gone.

You discover another startling fact as you shine the light over the floor.

Jacob Madd has vanished too.

Go to PAGE 66.

116

"I hope I don't regret this," you mutter. You follow Sam and Donny over the dune.

You gaze down and gasp. Below you are *hundreds* of cats!

Tall torches stand in a giant circle. The cats march around and around. They seem to be doing some kind of ceremonial dance. The torch flames cast long cat shadows across the beach.

A loud humming sound reaches you at the top of the dune. You listen for a moment. "Purring," you murmur.

Only it's not the purring of contented lap cats. This rumbling sound is louder and stronger. Menacing.

Terrifying.

Turn to PAGE 137.

"Now cut it out," you scold.

Together the twins pounce on you and attack you with the fur. "Stop it," you gasp, trying not to laugh. You are really annoyed — but the fur tickles.

Suddenly the door of the lighthouse opens. A flashlight beam floods the room. Three people step inside. It's your mom, your dad, and Katrina Madd.

"Mom! Dad!" you shout happily.

But they don't answer you. Or even glance at you.

"Well," your dad says, "I guess they're not in here."

"Of course they're not!" Katrina Madd snaps in annoyance. "I told you that already."

"Mom? Dad? We're right here," you say, waving your hand back and forth before their eyes.

You don't get it. They're acting as if you're all invisible! What's going on here?

Go to PAGE 94.

118

You don't want to waste any time. Those cats totally freak you out. "Come on." You start the climb up the spiral staircase.

Hmmm. You don't like the way the staircase rattles and sways. You don't like it at all.

"Be careful," you warn the twins. "This thing feels as if it's not attached to anything." You grab the railing, trying to balance yourself. The staircase shakes as if it's caught in an earthquake. Donny and Sam are holding their stomachs.

"Ugh!" Donny groans. "I'm going to be si-i-ick."

"Not on me you're not!" Sam cries from below Donny.

"Keep climbing!" you order them.

You clutch your own queasy stomach as one more swooping sway nearly knocks you off your feet. You step onto the tenth step.

Immediately the staircase starts spiraling like a giant corkscrew! And it's shrinking, taking you back down to the ground.

"Help!" you scream.

Go to PAGE 113.

"If that's Katrina Madd in the picture, then who did you meet?" Sam asks.

"I don't know," you murmur. Prickles of fear tingle on the back of your neck. You remember the cabdriver's warning: Watch out for Katrina Madd. You stare at the photo.

Could this be why? Is the woman you met an imposter? And does she have anything to do with these crazed cats?

"Let's see what else we'll find in this mess." You rifle through more papers.

Under a pile of articles about cats, you find two note cards clipped together. On one card there's a list of nine numbers. It looks as if it could be a locker combination or something. On the other card is a drawing of a spiral staircase. A circle is drawn around the tenth step. The word DOWN is written next to it.

You can't make sense of either card.

"There's nothing else here, guys," you say. "Let's just get out and try to go for help."

You're about to leave when you have second thoughts. Maybe those cards *do* mean something. Should you go back for them?

The shadowy figure of a cat glides across the floor.

They've gotten in somehow!

If you go back for the cards, turn to PAGE 46.

If you leave the cards and just get out, turn to PAGE 115.

120

"Let's go fishing," you decide. "We've never done that before."

"No fair," Sam mutters.

"I'm going to catch the biggest fish in the world!" Donny cries. He dashes into the store. You and Sam follow.

The store owner tells you about a good spot to fish just down the road. You find the pier easily. Very quickly you each catch several fish. You toss them into your fish pail.

"This is fun!" Donny exclaims.

"Uh-oh," Sam murmurs. "We have company."

You glance behind you. A dozen black cats sit at the other end of the pier. Watching.

Your stomach tightens. Are they really evil?

"What do you think they want?" Donny asks nervously.

"Maybe they're hungry." You toss them a piece of bait.

The cats pounce on it. They hiss at one another, fighting over the food.

Maybe that wasn't such a good idea, you realize.

Turn to PAGE 121.

The cats dash over to you, yowling. They turn your bait can upside down, spilling bits of fish onto the deck. They seem crazed with hunger.

More black cats swarm onto the pier. And more.

"Where are they all coming from?" Sam wails.

"Go away!" Donny screams as three cats knock him over.

"The fish!" you shout. You toss the fish to the army of cats. You hope this will make them leave you alone.

Instead it works them into a frenzy. They want more!

They knock over the rods. The fish pail. You!

They howl and meow, crawling all over you. They scratch at you, as if they think you're hiding food in your clothes.

They're going to rip me apart! you think in horror.

Then you spot a small motorboat tied to the pier. "Quick!" you tell Donny and Sam. "Down there. Let's get out of here!"

The twins leap into the boat. You toss out several hissing and spitting cats, then start the motor. You speed away from the dock as quickly as you can.

You can still hear the cats howling across the water.

Turn to PAGE 64.

The floor opens up just enough for the spiral to fit through.

"Where is it taking us?" Donny shrieks.

"Down!" Sam cries.

"No kidding!" you snap.

Sam peers down. "I want to get off!" he screams. "I don't want to go down into that cellar!"

Donny clutches the center pole that runs up through the middle of the staircase. "Let's jump!" he wails.

"Quiet!" you order. You're dizzy and scared too. And their screaming doesn't help you figure out what to do.

As scary as the deep black hole looks, that cellar could be a way to escape the cats.

Or it could lead to something even worse. Even an underground prison!

What should you do? Ride the spiral staircase down into the spooky basement where it's taking you? Or jump off now — risking your necks and running into the cats on the ground floor?

If you ride the spiral staircase all the way down, go to PAGE 113.

If you jump off now, turn to PAGE 97.

"Let's check out the house," you tell the twins. "Maybe we can find something that will help us."

You instruct the twins to search upstairs. You head for the garage. "Okay — what can we use to trap Katrina?" you mutter. You flick on the lights.

Your mouth drops open. This place is a cat paradise!

Cases of cat food fill floor-to-ceiling shelves. Sacks of cat litter line the walls. Cat toys sit in plastic tubs.

Hmmm. Tempt her with food? No, you decide. We'd have to open way too many cans for a cat that size.

You rummage through the cat toys. Aha! A rubber mouse on a string! No cat could resist it.

The twins burst into the garage. "Look what we found!" Donny cries. He and Sam hold up a large net hammock.

"We'll drop this on top of her," Sam announces. "She'll get all tangled up."

That could work too. . . .

So which will it be?

To lure Katrina into the garage using the rubber mouse, turn to PAGE 129.

To trap her in the hammock, turn to PAGE 34.

124

You pull out the drawing of the spiral staircase.

"Oh, no!" you groan. "This card won't help us at all."

Unless . . . you stare at it.

"Maybe it's a puzzle," you reason. "Maybe I have to find the other words hidden within the words 'SPIRAL STAIRCASE' or something."

It's worth a try, you decide.

How many words can you find? Use all the letters in SPIRAL STAIRCASE, in any order you like. Here's one word to get you started: CAT.

Now you start searching!

If you find nine or more words, go to PAGE 81.

If you find fewer than nine words, go to PAGE 100.

"This is definitely an emergency," you announce.

Holding your breath, you peel the tape off the envelope.

Nothing happens.

"Whew!" You exhale. "At least it didn't explode or anything!"

"What is it?" Sam demands. "Hurry up. Open it." Both he and Donny have their eyes glued to the envelope. You open the flap and dump the contents out into your shaking hand.

Huh? This is too weird. It's —

"Bubble gum!" you declare. You shake your head. You were ready for another booby trap. "What kind of emergency is bubble gum good for? This is ridiculous!"

"Well, maybe it's a snack attack emergency!" Donny exclaims. "I could sure use some bubble gum right now!"

"Me too," Sam agrees.

You hand over the pink gum to the twins. While they blow bubbles, you try to figure out what to do next.

You don't have long to think. Because you notice a flickering movement over by the window. A cat's tail.

Oh, no! You must have let a cat in with you when you opened the door. And all the traps have already been sprung!

Go to PAGE 106.

"We have to tell Mom and Dad," you insist. "What if Katrina comes to the house?"

Sam and Donny stare at you, openmouthed.

"You think she might?" Sam whimpers. Donny's face is completely white.

"It's possible," you mutter.

The three of you hurry along the path toward the house. Your senses are alert to all the night sounds — bushes rustling, wind whistling, footsteps.

Footsteps? The hairs on the back of your neck prickle. You pick up your pace.

So does the soft *PAD*, *PAD*, *PAD* of animal feet.

Turn to PAGE 99.

"Yaaaah!" You shriek as a hand clamps down on your shoulder.

In the ghostly glow of the flashing alarm lights, you see that the hand belongs to a wild-looking bearded man. His leathery fingers tighten their grip on you.

You struggle to free yourself. "Let go!" you yell.

Donny rushes forward and kicks your captor in the shin.

"Dag blast it!" the man shouts. He releases you and grabs his shin. You notice he's carrying a hose in his other hand. "You little monster," he snarls at Donny. "I told you to stay put!"

"Huh?" Donny stares at the wild man.

"No!" a voice calls from an iron spiral staircase in the middle of the room. "That was *me* you told to stay put."

"Sam!" you and Donny exclaim together.

Turn to PAGE 76.

Katrina's face flattens. Her ears shift to the top of her head. Her nose twitches as whiskers sprout out from under it. She lets out a wailing "Mrrrrrrrow!"

Her body trembles and shakes. Fur sprouts along her limbs. She lifts giant paws, flexing each claw. Her tail whips back and forth.

She is a giant white cat!

Once the transformation is complete, she shudders and crumples to the ground.

The cats stare at her. Waiting.

"Is she dead?" Sam whimpers.

"I — I don't think so," you stammer. You're not so sure.

As if to answer you, Katrina springs to her four feet. Her ears flick nervously, as if she's listening for something. Her nose lifts, sniffing the air.

The smaller cats surround her. You can't imagine what she's telling them.

All you know is, you don't want to stick around to find out!

Hurry over to PAGE 80.

"Trying to drop that thing on her is too risky," you decide. "We'll lure her into the garage with the mouse toy."

The twins grumble, but finally they agree.

"Here's what we'll do," you explain. "I'll go out and get her attention. Then I'll drag the mouse on the string and lead Katrina into the garage. Once she's inside I'll shut the door. She'll be trapped."

"Okay. What do *we* do?" Sam asked.

"Stay out of the way," you reply.

"No fair!" Donny complains.

"Okay, fine." You think for a second. "You guys will be in charge of shutting the garage door. From the outside. So keep hidden until she goes into the garage. Deal?"

Sam and Donny nod. "Deal," Donny says.

The twins dash back into the house. The inside door bangs shut behind them.

You're on your own. Your heart starts pounding.

What if Katrina is waiting on the other side of the garage door — ready to pounce?

Take a deep breath and slide open the garage door on PAGE 133.

130

You have to find out what Katrina and the cats are doing.

"Don't make a sound," you warn the twins. You lie down and peek over the dune. You lift your head only high enough to allow your eyes to clear the crest. Donny and Sam do the same.

Katrina kneels in the center of the circle. "I have done your bidding," she tells the cats. "My time as Keeper of the Cats is nearly over. As decreed, I am searching for the next Keeper."

What is she talking about? you wonder. She seems to think those cats can actually understand her.

Is she a total loony?

But then you notice the intent expressions on the faces of the cats. And you wonder if maybe Katrina is right.

In the next instant, something horrible starts to happen.

See what it is on PAGE 91.

Your eyes widen in horror. No wonder the cats all seemed to be after Jacob Madd! He's been holding them captive. Experimenting on them.

What a horrible man!

Jacob Madd steps forward, reaching for the twins.

"Leave them alone!" you shout. You shine the flashlight right into his eyes.

Madd is blinded long enough for you to open Katrina's cage. Katrina leaps out and tackles her brother. She scratches and claws like a cat, shouting at him in a furious human voice. "You're the evil one! Not the cats. You!"

Katrina Madd tears at her brother's face. The cats in their cages yowl fiercely.

Madd tries to protect himself with his arms, but Katrina shoves him into the cage she just left. Then she slumps to the floor, exhausted.

You rush to her side. Your eyes open wide in shock.

Fingers sprout from Katrina's paws. Her tail shrinks and vanishes. Her fur drops to the floor in huge clumps.

"She's dying," Sam gasps.

Go to PAGE 102.

132

"I think we should try to capture Katrina," you declare. "Then we'll use her to bargain with the army of cats."

"Awesome!" Sam exclaims. "But how will we catch her?"

"Yeah." Donny stares out the window at Katrina. "She's big and strong. And check out those teeth and claws."

Donny's right. It's not as if you are dealing with a regular little house cat. This is some kind of magical beast!

Still, as you study Katrina pacing in the yard, you can't help noticing how much like a regular cat she is.

So how can that help you?

Think about it all the way to PAGE 123.

VRROOOSSH! You slide open the garage door and peer out.

All clear.

You take a step and realize your legs are trembling. You force yourself to walk down the driveway.

You duck behind some bushes. Then you toss the mouse out into the middle of the driveway.

"Katrina!" you call. Your voice shakes. "Here, kitty, kitty."

The giant white cat bounds into view.

Cold fear travels up your spine. She's as big as a tiger! And just as powerful.

She stops at the sight of the mouse. You twitch the string gently. The mouse moves.

Katrina sinks to her haunches and begins to stalk it.

Straight toward you!

Turn to PAGE 26.

"Do something!" you shout to the twins.

"Gotcha!" Donny cries as he and Sam jump on the cat's back.

You back up to get out of the reach of his jaws. You feel buttons under your back. Uh-oh.

You must have backed into a control panel on the wall. And you have the worried feeling that you pressed every single one of those buttons.

Instantly, spotlights come on. Your eyes widen in shock.

All the stuffed cats in the room come to life at once! Their eyes light up like lasers.

The crippled tiger robot goes wild. He shakes the twins back and forth, trying to get rid of their weight. They clutch his fur as they are thrown up and down.

The army of mechanical cats marches toward you, forcing you deeper into your corner. The tiger flings the twins against the wall beside you.

Your screams mean nothing to this gang of robotic monsters. They feel nothing.

And when they're finished with you, you won't feel anything either . . . ever.

THE END

No matter how hard you think, you can't remember which step was circled. Donny and Sam can't remember either.

"Oh, well," you say at last. "Keep going. It probably didn't mean anything anyway." I hope, you think with a gulp.

You step onto the third step, then the fourth. Then you take them two at a time.

All three of you reach the tenth step at once.

The minute you hit that step, the spiral staircase spins down into the ground like a corkscrew.

"Hey!" you cry. "What's going on?"

"Hold on, Donny!" Sam shouts. "This thing is really sha-a-akkki-i-ing!"

"Heeelp!" Donny shrieks.

As the spiral staircase funnels downward at high speed you remember something:

It was the tenth step that was circled.

Go to PAGE 122.

So what if they think you're a wimp? You're *scared*!

You plant your feet in the sand. "No," you declare. "It's too dangerous! We have to get home."

"We want to go!" Sam wails.

Donny continues tugging your hand. "Please, please, please."

"Quit whining," you snap. "Or I'll tell Mom and Dad about the time —"

"Okay, okay," Donny mutters.

You trudge along the beach. The wind picks up again.

"Ow!" Sam complains. "The sand is going in my eyes."

"Bleh." Donny spits. "And in my mouth."

"Keep going," you order.

But the sandstorm is too powerful. For every step forward you take, it blows you and the twins three steps back.

Sand seeps into your clothes, weighing you down. You struggle on. But soon the horrible truth hits you.

You can't move anymore!

The sand continues blowing over you. In minutes, you, Donny, and Sam are completely buried.

You and your brothers are doomed to be duned!

THE END

Your heart pounds as you stare down at the bizarre tribe of cats. What are they doing?

You glance at Donny and Sam. They seem hypnotized by the pattern the cats make as they weave in and out of the torches.

More torches flare into flame. Someone must be down there. The cats couldn't have lit those torches!

Your eyes widen as you recognize the tall figure entering the circle. She carries two more lit torches into the center.

"That's Katrina Madd," you whisper.

"She looks kind of like a cat," Donny comments.

"You mean that's the lady who owns our house?" Sam cries.

Katrina suddenly glances up. Uh-oh. Did she hear Sam?

You yank Donny and Sam below the top of the dune. You hope she didn't see you. You have a feeling it would be bad if Katrina discovered you spying on her and the army of cats.

You want to stay to watch, but you're worried that they know you're there. You might be better off sneaking away now.

But maybe Katrina *didn't* see you. And you could find out what they're doing.

What should you do?

_____

If you think Katrina knows you're there, dash to PAGE 72.

If you want to stay and watch, hang out on PAGE 130.

About R.L. Stine

R.L. Stine is the most popular author in America.
He is the creator of the *Goosebumps*, *Give Yourself Goosebumps*, *Fear Street*, and *Ghosts of Fear
Street* series, among other popular books. He has
written nearly 200 scary novels for kids. Bob lives
in New York City with his wife, Jane, teenage son,
Matt, and dog, Nadine.